"DON'T S[...]"

Slocum warned. "I heard him say he doesn't carry a gun." He aimed for the cowboy's chest and came to a halt thirty yards away.

The cowboy gave him a steely-eyed stare. "Butt out of this, mister. Ain't none of your business."

"I'm making it my business," Slocum replied evenly. "I'll put a bullet right between your eyes unless you holster the gun and walk off. I don't give a damn what this is about, but you let him up and settle it some other way."

Very slowly, barely noticeable, the cowboy turned the barrel of his pistol in Slocum's direction.

"Don't try it!" Slocum snapped, readying his trigger finger for the moment when he sensed the other man meant to shoot. "I can't miss from here . . ."

DON'T MISS THESE
ALL-ACTION WESTERN SERIES
FROM THE BERKLEY PUBLISHING GROUP

THE GUNSMITH by J. R. Roberts
Clint Adams was a legend among lawmen, outlaws, and ladies.
They called him . . . the Gunsmith.

LONGARM by Tabor Evans
The popular long-running series about U.S. Deputy Marshal
Long—his life, his loves, his fight for justice.

SLOCUM by Jake Logan
Today's longest-running action Western. John Slocum rides
a deadly trail of hot blood and cold steel.

BUSHWHACKERS by B. J. Lanagan
An action-packed series by the creators of Longarm! The
rousing adventures of the most brutal gang of cutthroats ever
assembled—Quantrill's Raiders.

DIAMONDBACK by Guy Brewer
Dex Yancey is Diamondback, a southern gentleman turned
con man when his brother cheats him out of the family for-
tune. Ladies love him. Gamblers hate him. But nobody pulls
one over on Dex . . .

WILDGUN by Jack Hanson
Will Barlow's continuing search for his daughter, kidnapped
by the Blackfeet Indians who slaughtered the rest of his family.

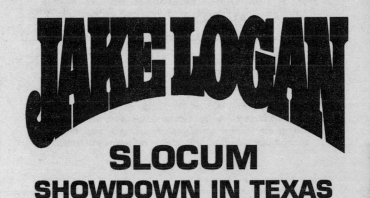

SLOCUM
SHOWDOWN IN TEXAS

J
JOVE BOOKS, NEW YORK

SHOWDOWN IN TEXAS

A Jove Book / published by arrangement with
the author

PRINTING HISTORY
Jove edition / January 2001

All rights reserved.
Copyright © 2001 by Penguin Putnam Inc.
This book, or parts thereof, may not be reproduced in any form
without permission.
For information address: The Berkley Publishing Group,
a division of Penguin Putnam Inc.,
375 Hudson Street, New York, New York 10014.

The Penguin Putnam Inc. World Wide Web site address is
http://www.penguinputnam.com

ISBN: 0-515-13000-1

A JOVE BOOK®
Jove Books are published by The Berkley Publishing Group,
a division of Penguin Putnam Inc.,
375 Hudson Street, New York, New York 10014.
JOVE and the "J" design
are trademarks belonging to Penguin Putnam Inc.

PRINTED IN THE UNITED STATES OF AMERICA

10 9 8 7 6 5 4 3 2 1

1

Austin had always been a violent city, with a reputation for being crowded with dangerous men. While many of them hid out along the Mexican border in places like Laredo or Eagle Pass in order to cross the Rio Grande ahead of the law when a bounty hunter or a Texas Ranger, or even a Federal Marshal got too close, away from the border, John Slocum knew of a few more tough Texas towns—Fort Worth and its Hell's Half Acre district, and Austin, built along the Colorado River. There was something about Austin that attracted wanted men; little law enforcement, despite the fact that it was the capital of Texas, and saloons full of beautiful women. A bottle of whiskey was what brought Slocum here. He was simply thirsty for a bottle of good Kentucky bourbon, and to replenish his supply of cheroots. He rode his bay stud into town with a watchful eye on everything, as if he almost knew trouble was close at hand. But he'd never been one to avoid trouble if it came straight at him. Riding through it was his way of doing things.

Austin's streets were busy with buggy traffic and *va-*

queros and drummers, including a fair number of working cowboys. A few drovers came to town simply to visit the girls and spend a night on the town. Pedestrians walked in front of store windows; women with parasols, children in tow, a handful of railroad trainmen moving to and from the depot over on First Street, as boilers were being filled, coal tenders taking on coal while passengers got on or off strings of pullmans and passenger cars. Farther up First Street lay the red light district, brothels for the working man and a few for the very rich. Slocum knew this town, although not well. He avoided it whenever he could because it seemed trouble always arrived in Austin at the same time he did.

He rode his stud to a livery stable and swung down with a grunt, feeling the miles he'd put under him since leaving the Mexican border. Working stiffness from his knees, he nodded to an aging liveryman chewing a length of straw as the man ambled out of his stable.

"Evenin', stranger. Name's Cobbs. I get four bits for a stall with good beddin' and a bait of grain. Clean water, too, an' my darkie stays here at night watchin' over things."

Slocum handed Cobbs a dollar in change. "Extra oats and the best stall you've got."

"Done, mister," Cobbs replied, grinning, revealing a few missing teeth. "This fine bay stallion will git the best treatment in town. I'll have Buck rub him down good, maybe put a trouch of linament on his forelegs. Looks like he's near 'bout road foundered."

"He's been a bunch of mighty rough, dry miles," Slocum agreed, remembering his ride up from Matamoros, stripping off his saddle. "I'll be staying at the Driskell Hotel. The name's John Slocum."

Cobbs frowned. "Seems like I've heard that name before," he said, sizing Slocum up with a cautious look. "Can't recall just exactly where."

"Not likely. I'm just passing through," Slocum replied as he carried his saddle to a tack shed in front of the barn. "I hardly ever visit this place. Too much gunplay, or so I hear."

"That's a natural fact," Cobbs said, taking the stud by the reins. "Worse now than ever. Meanest pack o' killers in town you ever saw—them Younger brothers, Clay an' Bob, has outright took over the Steamboat Saloon on Sixth Street. Sheriff Myers goes off fishin' whenever there's a ruckus so he don't have to face 'em. Word is, Lyle Sloan is runnin' with them Younger boys now, an' he's meaner'n two rattlers with a gun. If I was you I'd steer clear of the Steamboat while you're in town. Folks claim there's so many bullet holes in the roof it leaks like a sieve when it rains."

"Why doesn't your sheriff do something about it?" Slocum asked, pulling his Winchester .30-.30 from its rifle boot tied below a stirrup leather, shouldering his valise and rifle for a walk to the hotel.

"He scared to death of those varmits. John Myers ain't nobody's fool. He knows he can't stand up to 'em in a gunfight an' he can't recruit no deputies to side with him. In case you ain't acquainted with 'em, Clay Younger is 'bout the size of a grizzly bear, with a disposition to match. Bob is the quiet one, but he'd as soon back-shoot a feller as look at you. Now, ol' Red Sloan, they call him on account of his red hair, he's the worst. A paid shootist. Some say he's the quickest draw in the whole damn state, an' that covers a lot of territory in Texas."

"I reckon it does," Slocum said, turning toward the center of town. "I'll take your advice and stay wide of the Steamboat. No sense buying into trouble that ain't mine."

He trudged off carrying his gear and rifle, wondering if the liveryman could be right about the Younger brothers and Sloan. Men of their breed sometimes lived off oversized reputations, and when the chips were down, they proved to be ordinary men who bled and died just like everybody else.

A late afternoon sun slanted across LaVaca Avenue as he crossed the street, avoiding wagon and carriage traffic, taking note of a particularly pretty girl in a yellow dress carrying a parasol. Her skin was like ivory, tinted lightly across her face with rouge, and when she walked her bustle swayed back and forth hinting at what lay underneath it. Seeing her now, even as tired as he was, Slocum's sap went on the rise. Tonight he would look for a woman, after a hot bath and a shave and several straight shots of the city's best bourbon, then a big beefsteak.

He came to Fifth Avenue and entered the Driskell Hotel with every muscle in his body aching. He'd been five days in the seat of a saddle, sleeping in his bedroll while traveling open country, and he found himself looking forward to a soft mattress, feather pillows, some of the finer things.

"I need a room facing east, if you've got one, and a bath," he told a spectacled clerk.

"You're mighty particular, mister," the old man said, gazing at Slocum through thick lenses. "But I've got a good room facing the direction you want. Upstairs, number twenty-one. It'll be two dollars a night. How long did you aim to stay?"

"Depends," Slocum replied. "A couple of days at the most, if I find your bed comfortable and your bathwater hot."

"Bath house is at the back. Ida Lee, the colored woman, will take your clothes an' launder 'em for two bits, which includes the foldin' charge."

Slocum placed two dollars on the counter. The clerk palmed it and handed him a key.

"Sign the book," he said, pushing a register in front of Slocum. "Room's on the left, facin' east. Just curiosity, but why a room facin' east?"

"Always did enjoy a sunrise," he answered, signing his name on a blank line. "The day's gonna come when I won't see any more of 'em after I go to my grave and I hadn't planned on missing any while I've still got opportunity."

He picked up his gear and headed for the stairs, taking note of a sign reading "Bath House" at the end of a hallway. After he removed clean clothes from his valise, he meant to buy a bottle of whiskey and cigars before soaking in a hot bath tub, ridding his body of the aftermath of so many miles on a dusty trail.

He found room 21 and entered, placing his rifle in a corner before he unbuckled his gunbelt. The last of his weapons was hidden underneath his shirt—a .32 caliber bellygun. He tossed it on the bed and opened his valise, as weary as he ever remembered feeling.

"Old age, I reckon," he said to himself, wondering if it was possible that age and hard living were taking their toll on his frame.

Slocum was the only patron in Bill Tatum's Barber Shop at a quarter to five, getting a haircut and a shave after a luxurious bath and several shots of whiskey while soaking in the tub.

"You just passin' through?" his barber asked, trimming the short hair above his ears, making conversation.

"On my way to Denver, visiting a few old friends

along the way. Ranchers, mostly. Otherwise I'd be taking the train. Austin just happened to be where sundown caught up to me."

"This is a friendly town, for the most part."

"If I was looking for a pretty lady to spend an evening with where would I go?" Slocum asked.

"If you're askin' about a woman for hire, the prettiest ones are at Anna's on Sixth Street. Just look for a big white-washed building with a red lamp hangin' next to the front door. Tell whoever answers the door that you're lookin' for Anna."

"I wasn't exactly meaning a woman for hire, but I may give Anna's a try. How about a quiet drinking parlor where a woman might allow a gentleman to buy her a drink?"

The barber wagged his head. "That used to be the Steamboat before a bad element came to town. A bunch of hired guns took over the place a few weeks back. Our sheriff ain't got a lick of backbone . . . won't stand up to 'em. They tell me he asked for help from the Texas Rangers an' United States Marshals, only ain't any Rangers showed up till now. There's been plenty of bloodshed at the Steamboat. Folks with good sense don't go there no more. Just last week four gents got hauled out of there feet first."

"The liveryman was telling me about it. He made mention of a couple of brothers, and some shootist by the name of Sloan."

Now the barber scowled. "Red Sloan. He's cold-blooded mean, they tell me. The brothers are named Younger. Come from up in Missouri. Ex-Confederates, so the stories go. I sure wouldn't advise you to try the Steamboat lookin' for a woman, or a drink neither. A man could get killed just walkin' through them swingin' doors."

"It doesn't sound like Austin's got much of a sheriff," Slocum observed dryly. "He should form a posse and go in there to clean the place out."

"It'd be hard to find anybody for that posse, mister. This town ain't exactly full of folks lookin' for an early grave. We elected ourselves a sheriff, only nobody knew he'd turn out to be chicken-livered. He made citizens a bunch of fancy promises, only he ain't hardly kept a single one. Nobody really wants his job. The last feller who wore that badge got his head blown off by a shotgun blast when he tried to end a disturbance at the It'll Do Club. The city council called for a special election an' nobody ran for the sheriff's office, 'cept for John Myers. It don't pay much . . . not nearly enough to be worth gettin' killed over."

Slocum smelled bay rum hair tonic being massaged into his scalp, then the barber began combing his hair. An old memory surfaced. "I recollect there being a Ranger Post here not too many years ago."

"Closed it down temporarily, on account of all the Comanche troubles out west. Not enough Rangers to go around, they said. So if you're headed northwest toward Denver, you keep your eyes open for Injuns. They've gone on a bloody rampage out there, so the newspaper says."

He'd been aiming to ride cross-country to the South Fork of the Bosque to see Wayland Burke, a rancher in McLennan County and an old friend from the war. "I'll do that," he said idly, with an eye on the barber shop's front windows. "I wouldn't care to waste a good haircut by gettin' scalped so soon afterward, if I can help it."

The barber chuckled as he unfastened his sheet from around Slocum's neck, brushing down his sleeves with a tiny wisk broom. "Go up Sixth Street. Anna's place is on the right-hand side of the road. You can't miss it.

There'll be a red conductor's lantern hangin' on the porch, so everybody'll know what type of business she's in."

"I'm obliged," Slocum said as he swung out of the chair to hand over a fifty cent piece, taking his gunbelt and coat and his stetson from a hat rack near the door.

"Don't forget what I said about the Steamboat, mister," the barber reminded. "I see you're packin' a gun, but unless you fancy yourself a real quick-draw artist, I'd stay away from that place."

Slocum smiled, buckling on his gun. "I'm not looking for a place where I can step in front of a bullet, so thanks for the warning."

He walked out just as a pretty woman with fiery red hair was passing the barber shop. She was wearing a soft blue gown, open at the neck. He nodded politely and said, "Evening, ma'am."

She smiled demurely and averted her eyes. "Good evening to you, sir," she replied softly, her cheeks showing a sudden flush. She hurried past him, but as she continued down the street she glanced over her shoulder and found him looking at her.

He tipped his hat and grinned again, which only worsened her embarrassment when she knew he saw her backward glance. Turning her head quickly, she walked even faster to a street corner and disappeared around it.

"Austin's got its good points," he said under his breath as he turned for an eatery he remembered being close to the river, the lower Colorado, a place where he'd enjoyed a good steak during previous visits. He strolled casually down the street, nodding to some of the city's beautiful women, when they were not in the company of a gentleman or a child. It was true . . . Austin had a goodly number of remarkably pretty girls, he thought.

Nearing a bridge crossing the river, he happened to see a sign hanging above the doors to a big building with a pair of bat wings covering the entrance. He stopped when he was directly in front of the Steamboat.

He sauntered past after only a brief hesitation. No sense buying into trouble.

2

Her name was Myra Reed, she said. She brought him bourbon in a crystal shot glass and smiled when she placed it on the table.

"That'll be forty cents, Mr. Slocum," she said, blonde hair hanging loosely over her bare shoulders. She wore a pale blue blouse, revealing a portion of her ample bosom. Her eyes seemed to glitter in light from a glass lamp fixture hanging from the ceiling.

"Thank you," he said, placing a dollar on her tray. "Please keep the change. This is a nice place, just what I was looking for, a drinking establishment where I can enjoy myself in peace and quiet." Glancing around before the girl left his table, he counted three other patrons at the bar. A sign above the doorway drew him here, to The Cattlemen's Club on LaVaca Street. Out in front, a Studebaker carriage with a canopy was parked next to the doorway with a driver waiting in the front seat. Slocum had eaten a steak and fried potatoes at the Capitol Cafe on Congress Avenue, and some of his trail weariness had ebbed away.

"Our drinks are more expensive, but the liquor is

good," she said, smiling in a slightly suggestive way. She wore a full length skirt, hiding the shape of her legs but not the swell of her rounded hips. "Some places serve watered-down whiskey, or a carmel-colored home-brew. We serve only the best. It's Wednesday, so it'll be a slow night."

He tasted his bourbon and found it an almost perfect blend of distilled barley and corn mash. "It's delicious. And if you pardon me for saying so, it tastes much better in the company of a pretty lady. You're a very beautiful woman."

She did not blush or look away. "Thank you, sir," she said with a nod and a smile.

He looked deeply into her blue eyes. "I'm quite sure a woman with your good looks has a regular suitor," he added, seeking the information he wanted as he sipped from his glass a second time.

"I have a gentleman friend, but it's nothing serious. I'm very choosy about the company I keep."

"I had no doubts. And please call me John."

She put her tray down when she saw no other customer needed attention. "What sort of business are you in?" she asked, still with a touch of reserve in her voice, making small talk.

"I dabble in several things. On occasion I do a little bit of detective work for the railroads. I buy and sell livestock, mostly blooded horses."

"Detective work?"

He nodded.

"That sounds exciting. And dangerous, I suppose."

"Not really. It's only dangerous if you're careless."

Her gaze fell to the outline of the pistol beneath his coat and she said, "You carry a gun."

"I rarely ever need one," he replied, which was only part truth. He didn't want to frighten her.

"What kind of detective work?" she asked.

"Sometimes I help locate stolen cattle and horses. Once in a while I work for the railroads after a robbery. I've done some investigative work for a few banks."

"You're not from around here. Where do you live?"

"I stay close to Denver most of the time these days, but I'm a man who likes to travel. See the country. Right now I'm on my way back to Denver, but not on pressing business. A gentleman I'm acquainted with there is interested in some blooded race horses I bought in Mexico."

"Then you move around a lot," she said.

"At times, however I prefer a more settled life. If I could find the right place, and maybe the right woman, I might put down some roots." It was what women looking for a man wanted to hear, and he knew it from years of experience, seducing beautiful girls in town after town during his travels.

She tilted her head. "And just what is the 'right woman' made of?" she asked, smiling. "I've never met a man who knew."

He downed half his drink and toyed with the glass as though he was momentarily deep in thought. "She has to be pretty, and have an understanding nature when it comes to a man's . . . urges."

"Urges?"

"The natural kind, if you know what I mean. When a man is needing a woman—"

"You can be very forward, Mr. Slocum."

"Please call me John, and I meant no offense by the remark. You asked what the right woman is made of."

Myra's smile widened. "So I did, John. And you wasted no time telling me what it was, in your opinion."

"I believe in honesty between a man and a woman. It's such a waste of time, playing games."

"And are you playing games with me?" she asked, lowering her voice so patrons and the bartender could not hear.

"Not at all. I'm only being honest."

"It almost sounds like an indecent proposition was made to me just now."

"Nothing indecent about a man and woman being together, in my judgment," he said.

Her tone turned husky. "Do you mean when they are together in the same bed?"

"That's one way of being together. There are others. Let me assure you I meant no offense."

"None was taken, John. I was only wondering . . ."

He emptied his glass. "I'm wondering if you'd like to have a drink with me later on, perhaps a bottle of good brandy or some cognac."

"I have to work until midnight, even on nights when it's slow, like tonight."

"What would you say if I told you I'll be waiting for you out front with a bottle of your favorite spirits? I'll rent a carriage at the livery and we can go for a moonlight drive along the river, perhaps."

"You'll think I'm a cheap woman if I agree."

"No ma'am. I'll know you're an honest lady who is interested in spending some time with me while we get to know each other. Nothing else was meant or implied."

"If I agree to go with you, you won't make inappropriate advances?" Myra asked. "You're a stranger. We just met a few moments ago. I know almost nothing about you, except what you've told me."

"You have my word as a gentleman that I will not make any inappropriate advances."

"How do I make certain you are a gentleman?"

He got out of his chair and looked down at her. "I'll

meet you out front at midnight. I'll prove to you that I'm a gentleman and a man of my word."

"I'll be taking an awful chance—"

"Please tell me what you'd like in the way of refreshments."

She hesitated. "I do like the sweet taste of good cognac so very much . . ."

She wore a light shawl around her bare shoulders when she came outside. Fall brought cooler temperatures to the Colorado River bottomlands at night.

"A pleasant evening, Miss Reed," he said, stepping down to assist her into the carriage. He offered her his hand. "Almost a full moon, which should make the river drive even more pleasant at this time of night."

"I really shouldn't do this," she said, halting at the edge of the running boards, trying to read Slocum's face in the dark. "I'm expected at home. I live with my aunt and she's not well. Perhaps we should do this some other time."

"I can drive you home whenever you wish. Although I did buy a bottle of imported French cognac. You can sample it on the way home."

She looked at the buggy. "You went to all the expense of renting a carriage. I suppose no harm will be done if we went for a short drive . . ."

She allowed him to assist her into the buggy, and when she was settled, he walked around the back and climbed in beside her to take the reins.

"The cognac and glasses are in a basket under the seat. If you'll do the honors by pulling the cork, we'll drive slowly so as not to spill any. Tell me which direction to go."

She appeared thoughtful. "There is a lane running beside the river northwest. We could take a short ride that way, but you must promise you'll take me home whenever I ask you to. I will not agree, otherwise."

"Consider it done, then," he said, shaking reins over the back of a brown gelding.

The buggy rolled away from The Cattlemen's Club at a slow walk down an empty street, for the hour was late.

Myra took the cognac from the basket beneath the seat and opened it, having some difficulty pouring into glasses Slocum had bought at a shop selling tobacco and fine wines. She handed him the glass and he drank from it while she poured one for herself, despite the buggy's bumpy ride.

"It's a nice night," he said, to begin conversation as they drove to the outskirts of Austin.

"Very nice," she said. "A bit cool, but far better than the heat of summertime."

"You look lovely tonight," he said. "This moonlight does something to your hair."

"You say the sweetest things, John. Are you trying to be a gentleman, or do you mean what you said?"

"I mean every word. I'm not one to pass off idle talk in serious matters."

Myra drank deeply from her glass. "This is very good, Mr. Slocum, not a cheap brand."

He swung the buggy horse down a wooded lane when they came to the river. "I've made it a practice to avoid cheap things. I like expensive cigars, expensive horses, and classy women."

She turned to him. "You think I'm classy?" she asked, and when she did, she gave him a coy smile. "Or is that just a line you give every woman you meet?"

He had to be sure she understood what he meant. "There are all kinds of women. Some can be very poor and still have as much class as a rich lady. Class comes from inside, not the clothes you wear or how much money you have in the bank."

She listened to the soft plop of the horse's hooves for a time, thinking about what he said. "It's true, I think. Money can't buy respectability—" Something caught her eye in front of the carriage. "Over there, John. There's a place where you can turn around, right by that big oak tree."

"You want me to take you home now?" he asked, pulling back on the reins.

She gave him a lingering look. "If that's what you want," she told him. "It's chilly out here in the dark and I didn't bring a coat, only this shawl."

He turned the horse around. "I'm staying at the Driskell Hotel. Would you care to join me there for one last drink before I drive you home?"

"It wouldn't seem proper," she replied, draining her glass of cognac before she poured another for both of them, smiling as she returned the cork to the neck of the bottle. "A woman who is concerned about her reputation shouldn't be seen entering a man's hotel room after dark."

"There are stairs at the back next to the bath house," he said gently. "No one would see you."

She stared into his eyes. "You presume that I would agree to go there?"

He rested the reins over the dashboard and took her in his arms, speaking softly now. "I only presume that a man and a woman should be honest about their intentions, Miss Reed. If you find my suggestion inappropriate I will apologize and take you straight home."

Myra said nothing for several seconds, examining his face in light from the moon. "I also believe in honesty, John. If you won't think any less of me, then we can go up to your room for a drink . . ."

He tightened his embrace, but only slightly, and then gave her a light kiss on the lips. "I will only think more of you for being an honest woman," he said, releasing her shoulders to grip the reins.

He slapped the gelding across its rump and turned back for Austin under a sky sprinkled with stars. Myra moved closer to him on the buggy seat and rested one slender hand on his thigh while she tipped back her glass with the other.

He felt a stirring in his groin, the pulsing beginnings of an erection. He urged the buggy horse to a slow trot, wondering what Myra would look like without her clothes. A sixth sense told him she was ready now, despite her protestations.

"Why are you asking the horse to hurry?" she asked, jolted by the increased pace of the carriage wheels.

When he glanced at her, she was smiling. "Because I think we've wasted enough time under the stars," he said. "Besides, I promised the liveryman I'd have his horse back before two o'clock in the morning."

"But what about driving me home?" Myra asked, flashing her perfect white teeth in a smile.

He didn't answer her, for she already knew the answer. He would take her home sometime after sunrise.

3

When he began taking off her corset he found the bindings tight, too restrictive to allow his fingers room to work, and he had trouble with knots on laces across the front after placing her blouse across a straight-backed chair at one side of the bed. Myra moaned, her face illuminated by pale moon light from the window.

"You promised me you wouldn't do this . . ." she mumbled under the strong influence of cognac, her words slightly mushy. He'd had to help her up the rear stairway, steadying her with an arm around her waist while she giggled over her poor balance when she lost her footing.

Slocum unfastened the knot and pulled strings off the hooks holding her undergarment in place. "I promised not to make any inappropriate advances. Don't you think this is appropriate?"

"I thought you were a gentleman . . ." She giggled softly.

"I am a gentle man. I'll show you just how gentle I can be under any circumstances, if that's what you want."

"Your . . . cock is so big. I can feel it against my leg when you rub against me. It's so big I'm sure it will hurt. Please don't hurt me with it."

"I promise I'll be gentle, just a little bit at a time until you tell me to stop."

"And what if I don't ask you to stop?" She giggled again.

He pushed the corset down, across her hips, past her knees until the garment fell at the foot of the bed. "Then I won't stop," he promised.

Her breathing became faster when his hand moved gently over the mound of soft hair at the tops of her thighs. "It feels so good when . . . you touch me, John. But I want you to stop. I must go home now. My aunt is waiting up for me and she'll worry."

"You can tell your aunt something unexpected came up," he said, taking her hand, placing it so her fingers curled around the thickness of his shaft where it strained against his undershorts.

A moan, a mixture of pleasure and fear, escaped her lips. "I'm quite certain I won't tell Aunt Nell what it was that came up," she said in a husky voice, slowly stroking his member. "I can't tell her about this . . ."

He cupped one creamy breast with a palm and gently rolled her nipple between his thumb and forefinger. She gasped and a tiny shudder coursed down the length of her body. "Oh, John," she whispered. "Take off your shorts so I can feel your cock with my fingertips."

He obliged her while lying on his side, tossing his shorts to the floor. Her hand encircled his prick, and when it did she let out another gasp. "I've never seen . . . I've never felt one so big! Even if I were to decide to let you make love to me, this wouldn't fit inside me . . . I just know it wouldn't fit."

He grinned. "I'd never be one to push you to such a

decision, Myra, but let me assure you that if you did decide to make love to me, I'll put it in very gently, not all of it, you understand." He pinched her rosy nipple a little harder, and suddenly her spine arched off the mattress.

"It's too big around to go in at all," she groaned, fingers measuring his circumference unconsciously while she kept pumping up and down on his cock. "I'm afraid it will tear me in half. I won't let you hurt me that way, but I do wish there was something we could do . . ." She trembled and fell back on the bed with a sigh, still jacking his prick, moaning, moving her head side to side on the pillow with her eyes tightly closed.

Slocum put a finger between the moist lips of her cunt and gently entered her, feeling her slick wetness and the fever in her loins. He was sure he could work his cock into her if he did it slowly, without too much pressure.

Involuntarily, she began hunching against his finger as tiny spasms gripped her thighs. "Please John," she whimpered. "You must think of something. I feel like I'm about to explode."

He withdrew his wet finger and moved carefully between her legs, placing the tip of his cock against her mound.

"No, John!" she cried, grinding her pelvis up and down as she held firmly to his cock with her fingers. "It's much too big."

With only the slightest pressure he pushed his prick between the lips of her cunt and now, as she thrust herself against his cock he saw a tear glisten on her cheeks.

"I want it," she whispered, "but there isn't room. You have the biggest prick . . . too large for a girl like me. I'm not very experienced . . ."

Ever so slowly he pressed his member slightly deeper until it would go no further, meeting resistance. And still, Myra ground her tight opening back and forth, making a wet, sucking sound when the tip of his prick went in and out.

"You must stop," she gasped, releasing her grip on his cock to encircle his buttocks with both hands, clawing fiercely into his skin with her fingernails, pulling him closer, deeper.

The irony did not escape him, her protests and her hunger for his prick, asking him to stop while she drew him closer to her, gyrating her hips, thrusting forward with her wet cunt at the same time she told him to end it.

"Just a little more," he whispered, scenting the sweet smell of her hair, her lilac perfume.

"No. Please no," she hissed, clenching her teeth yet with an ever-increasing tempo to her pelvic thrusts, again voicing a wish for him to stop while her body seemed to be demanding more of his prick. "You said you were a gentleman—"

"I'll do it gently," he replied, pushing harder, feeling the muscles in her cunt relax, opening a fraction more to accept his cock.

"That . . . feels . . . good," she breathed, "but you simply must stop. You're hurting me."

"You said it felt good."

"It does. It hurts, and it feels good. I don't understand it. Oh, please stop before you hurt me any more."

Slocum had known for years he would never be able to understand women. "There's such a thing as hurting in a good way?" he asked, pumping gently, more deeply, into her opening. Slippery sounds accompanied their every move and the heat from her cunt was like a fire.

"Yes. I mean . . . no." Her fingernails dug deeper into his buttocks. Tiny beads of sweat formed on her brow and the cleft between her breasts.

His erection was throbbing and the warm wetness around it caused his balls to rise, spreading a warmth of their own down his thighs, across his abdomen. He could smell her sweet musk and the tremors in her limbs only added to his excitement. He pushed deeper inside her, and suddenly her body went rigid underneath him.

"Now," she sighed, hammering against his shaft in spite of a lingering trace of resistance where the walls of her hungry cunt held him back. "Please stop now—"

He closed his mind to her feeble protests and thrust a half inch more of thick cock into her.

"Oh John . . . no more. I can't take any more."

The bed began to rock, bedsprings squeaking. The headboard banged the wall of the room with every stroke and he was sure that any second now, his testicles would explode.

Her breathing came in short bursts and soft sounds arose in her throat. "John—John—John."

Her skin had grown so clammy he found he was barely able to stay on top of her, the friction between their bodies creating more sweat, matting the thick hair on his chest. Her breasts swayed with every stroke, rotating against his ribs like giant mounds.

Without warning her cunt opened, and despite his promise to be gentle with her he buried his member inside her almost all the way to the hilt.

Myra screamed, clawing his buttocks until he felt blood run down his sides—she arched her spine, shaking violently, as the echo of her scream became a wail, then a softer groan. And all the while she continued to thrust against the base of his shaft with powerful lunges, hammering against him, his balls slapping the crack of her ass as he pounded his cock into her womb more rapidly.

She slammed her groin into him several more times

and then her entire body went rigid. She wailed, digging her heels into his calves, rising off the bed with him on top of her in spite of his weight.

As she reached her climax, his testicles spewed forth a stream of jism and the feeling of ecstasy was so intense that he let out a groan, driving his cock into her at tremendous speed and with the full force of the muscles in his hips.

"Oh God!" she shouted, cords of muscle standing out in her neck, her arms clasped around him with surprising strength for a small girl.

She collapsed on sweat-soaked bed sheets, panting, completely out of breath. Her head lolled to one side on the pillow and for a time she was motionless, her limbs falling limply on the mattress. She gasped for breath.

He spent the rest of his jism in her as gently as he could and then halted the thrusting motion of his cock, finding he was also short of breath. Resting on his elbows so she could breathe, he looked down at her in the moonlight spilling from the window.

"You're really some special kind of woman, Myra," he said. "I never felt anything quite like this."

Her eyes fluttered open. She stared at him a moment. "You bastard," she said softly. "You promised me you would stop if I asked you to."

"I meant to stop, only you felt so good . . . it felt so good being inside you that I couldn't help myself."

A slow smile crossed her face. "I knew you were a liar the minute I set eyes on you. Men who lie to women have a certain look about them."

"I'm sorry if I disappointed you."

Her smile changed to a mock scowl. "You hurt me. Your cock was too big and you used it anyway."

"Like I said, I just couldn't help it. And you didn't say a man has to be perfect, did you? Sometimes men are overwhelmed by emotion. It's a human characteristic. I'm only a man, and if a beautiful woman winds up in my bed I can't always control some of my urges."

"You lied to me." She said it playfully, not with reproach in her voice.

"I simply forgot what I said in a moment of passion. I hope you won't hold it against me."

She stirred underneath him, and the movement brought a smile to her lips. The muscles in her thighs quivered. She kissed him hard across the mouth and he sensed her hunger was about to come alive again.

Very gently, he moved his prick inside her, pulling back as if he meant to withdraw. She reached for him to hold him where he was.

"Don't leave yet," she whispered. "I like the way it feels now, when your cock isn't so hard."

"I hadn't planned on leaving, my darling. Just a change in my position, is all."

Her groin tensed and he could feel a tightening around his prick.

"I want more," she said huskily, "only please don't put it in me so deeply."

He began slow strokes in and out, and now the wet, sucking sounds were louder than before with her juices mingling with his jism.

"Like that," she sighed, closing her eyes, wrapping her arms around his back.

His slow pumping aroused her further, and her limbs began to tremble again.

"Not too deep," she groaned, wincing slightly as if the pain had also reawakened within her downy mound.

Slocum continued his shallow strokes, feeling his member thicken again, and at the same time her cunt opened slightly to allow him deeper penetration.

"Faster," she whispered in his ear, increasing the pressure of her embrace as her fingernails dug into his back. Again the bed began to squeak as their passion mounted.

"Faster," Myra cried, gasping, curling her legs around his to hold him in a viselike grip.

He felt a pulse in his cock. Her cunt was so slippery and wet that despite his second promise not to drive his prick into her too deeply, he found himself out of control. When she bowed her back off the mattress, seeking more of him, he obliged her and sent his prick all the way to the hilt.

"Oh yes!" Myra exclaimed, clawing his back fiercely. "Do it harder . . . faster."

He let go of all his reserve and began hammering his cock into her pussy, feeling the lips of her cunt stretch to accept him. Her juices flowed down his balls, warm and slick.

"Now!" she cried, rocking against him with so much force he had to cling to each corner of the mattress to stay atop her, seeking a purchase in the bedsheet with his toes.

"Yes! Yes! Yes!" she screamed, her body turning to iron beneath him when a second climax overwhelmed her.

His balls erupted a few moments later, and it seemed to him that the room was spinning . . .

4

One of the first signs of winter came on gusts of wind as he walked toward the livery to check on his horse, remembering Myra and her wonderful, passionate cries during the night. She was like a lot of women he'd known, protesting innocence of any desire for a man while she led him on, teasing him, allowing him to go farther while denying it was what she wanted. He knew in the end she would desire him as much as he desired her, and as it turned out she became demanding, asking for more until they were both completely spent. He'd taken her home not long after dawn, renting the carriage again from a sleepy-eyed livery worker, then driving across town with Myra resting her head contentedly against his shoulder. They agreed to spend another night together and thus his plans to leave Austin for the upper Bosque River country were delayed . . . delightfully delayed by a woman who wanted him between her thighs instead of on the trail toward McLennan County. John's friend would understand. Back in the war years they had formed a deep and lasting friendship as they fought side by side and sought pleasures in the same fashion when time and circumstance allowed. Like Slocum, Burke had boyish good looks and he knew how to use them to seduce a maiden if opportunity came knocking for a lonely soldier, which it rarely did during those trying times when a man never knew if a particular day might be his last.

Slocum entered the livery and inspected the bay, finding the stud with a bucket of clean oats and good bedding straw.

"He's happy as a pig in the mud," Cobbs said, chewing a cud of tobacco. "I tol' you I'd see he got took good care of an' I'm a man of my word, 'specially when it comes to horses. A man has to know how to take care of good stock."

"I'm well satisfied," Slocum said, turning away from the stall. "I'll be staying another night." He grinned. "I met a lady at The Cattlemens' Club, one of the prettiest creatures I ever laid eyes on."

Cobbs knitted his brow, a look of concern. "Wouldn't be a woman by the name of Myra Reed would it?" he asked, and by his tone Slocum knew something was wrong.

"That's her name, for a fact. Why do you ask?"

Cobbs looked around the barn quickly, as if to make sure no one else was listening. "She keeps company now an' then with Red Sloan, the feller I tol' you about yesterday. He fancies her bein' his woman, an' I'd sure as hell hate to cross trails with him over some female, or for any damn reason. He's one of the fastest guns in these parts an' he's got a temper to go with it, a real vicious disposition, if you know what I mean. If I was you I'd leave Myra plumb alone. She's a right pretty little thing, all right, but she ain't worth dyin' for. Comes from a poor family . . . her aunt's got the consumption. Sloan is a hell of a gambler an' he gives her money, or so I hear. He figures he's done bought an' paid for her."

Slocum glanced out at the sunlit street. "She told me she had a suitor, but it wasn't anything serious."

"It could get real serious if Red Sloan finds out you've been courtin' his woman, Mr. Slocum. It could get deadly serious over somethin' like that."

Slocum smiled inwardly, recalling last night's wild romp on the hotel bed with Myra. "If she tells me she doesn't care to see me again, I'll keep riding. But unless I hear it from her that she's spoken for, I fully intend to see her again while I'm in town."

"That could be a real serious mistake," Cobbs warned. "If you intend to make good on that promise, maybe you'd best tell me who to contact about this here bay stud if you happen to wind up in a pine box."

Slocum sauntered to the stable doors. "I don't figure that'll be necessary, Mr. Cobbs, but in the unlikely event anything happens to me, you can keep the stud. I can see you know how to care for good horses."

Cobbs caught up to him and looked him squarely in the eye. "You're either mighty brave or mighty dumb," he said with a note of disbelief in his voice. "I guess you ain't heard about Red Sloan or you wouldn't be talkin' so all-fired crazy. Back when he first come to town late in the summer, he went up against Joe Tucker. Tucker was just about the meanest son of a bitch with a gun this town ever saw—had five notches in his gun an' some say he killed a bunch more men down on the border. Ol' Red Sloan drew against him over a card game, a full house with Aces high when Tucker had a pair of Aces himself. Now, you don't need to be no expert at countin' to know there ain't but four Aces in a deck of cards. By the table count, there was five an' Tucker called Sloan a cheat. Sloan stood up an' called Tucker a damn liar, an' if he believed he'd been cheated he could go for his damn gun any time he took the notion. A friend of mine, Alvin Weeks, he was there an' seen the whole thing. Tucker went for his gun first, only Sloan came up with iron in his fist before Tucker could clear leather."

When Cobbs hesitated, Slocum asked, "So Sloan fired first and killed Tucker?"

Cobbs looked down at his shoes. "Wasn't quite like that, but nearly so. Sloan shot first, only he missed on account of he was so damn drunk. Tucker took a shot, an' he missed same as Sloan because he was drunk, too. But Sloan, he got it right the second time. He aimed real careful an' blowed Tucker out of his damn boots. Slug went right through his gizzard."

Slocum nodded, for he understood. "That's the way it is in the gunfighter's trade, mostly. A man gets a reputation he ain't earned. Tucker was too slow, and this Sloan gent had bad aim. I imagine I've seen a couple dozen owlhoots just like 'em. In any gunfight, the only thing that matters is who can hit what he's aiming at first. Quickness isn't everything and more often than not, it'll get a man killed because he didn't take time to aim."

Cobbs narrowed his eyelids. "You sound like you know a thing or two 'bout gunfightin', Mr. Slocum. I reckon I hadn't oughta ask, but are you a shootist by profession? I seen right off when you came to town you was wearin' that cross-pull rig, an' that's damn near always the mark of a shooter."

"I make a habit of avoiding gunplay," he replied. "I wear a cross-draw holster for convenience. You have me figured wrong."

The liveryman still appeared doubtful. "You sure seem to know plenty about the subject." He shrugged. "Hell, I don't suppose it matters if'n you're aimin' to stay wide of Sloan an' them Younger boys. Only, that woman's liable to set off a few sparks if Sloan finds out you been courtin' her."

"I'll be leaving town tomorrow," Slocum said.

Cobbs cast a glance toward the Steamboat Saloon farther down the street. He wagged his head. "That may not be soon enough, my friend, if Sloan gets word you're seein' Myra."

Slocum tipped his hat to the stableman and walked out into brilliant afternoon sunshine, feeling a slight chill in the winds whipping through Austin from the north. He turned for the cafe, no longer thinking about the gunmen at the Steamboat, worrying that a cold spell might catch him on the trail to Burke's ranch and that would mean several miserable nights huddled around a camp fire.

As he was nearing the river he heard a commotion, angry voices coming from a side street. When he came to the corner he looked that way, halting at the edge of the boardwalk to watch what was taking place.

A lanky cowboy in a canvas duster and sweat-stained felt stetson was standing over a man lying on his back in the roadway, and the cowboy wearing the duster had a gun in his hand. The brim of his hat was pulled low in front, covering his eyes. He had a prominent Adam's apple and long ropelike arms. His gun was aimed down at the younger man beneath him.

"You're a lyin' son of a bitch!" the cowboy snarled.

"I never sleeved no Queen!" the young boy protested. "I drew it fair an' square. You've got no call to pull a gun on me an' bust me over the head with it. I won the pot an' you know it well as me."

"I say you're a goddamn liar, boy. I'm gonna shoot a hole plumb through both of them dishonest hands, so you'll remember not to cheat at cards."

"I didn't cheat you. I drew the third Queen honest when the dealer called for cards."

Slocum watched the cowboy cock his revolver.

"Please don't shoot me!" the boy cried. "I ain't even got a gun. You'll be shootin' an unarmed man—"

"I'll be puttin' holes through a goddamn card cheat," the cowboy answered, aiming for one of the younger man's palms.

It wasn't Slocum's affair and he knew it, but he wasn't made to stand by and let some bully shoot a man who didn't have a gun. He turned up the street and opened his coat, pulling his Colt .44 as he approached them.

"Don't shoot the boy!" Slocum warned. "I heard him say he doesn't carry a gun." He aimed for the cowboy's chest and came to a halt thirty yards away.

The cowboy gave him a steely-eyed stare. "Butt out of this, mister. Ain't none of your business."

"I'm making it my business," Slocum replied evenly. "I'll put a bullet right between your eyes unless you holster the gun and walk off. I don't give a damn what this is about, but you let him up and settle it some other way."

Very slowly, barely noticable, the cowboy turned the barrel of his pistol in Slocum's direction.

"Don't try it!" Slocum snapped, readying his trigger finger for the moment when he sensed the other man meant to shoot. "I can't miss from here—"

The cowboy stared at him, and Slocum returned his hard look. They watched each other, and now several pedestrians stopped on the boardwalks to witness what was taking place.

"Maybe you don't know who I am," the cowboy said, his voice like a rasp across cold iron.

"I don't give a damn who you are," Slocum replied,

"and it won't matter except to the undertaker who has to carve your name on your tombstone."

"I'm Bob Younger. Don't that ring a bell in your thick skull?"

"No bells. I figure I'm looking at a yellow son of a bitch, is all, a man who'd shoot an unarmed man. I don't give a damn what you call yourself, or who you claim to be. *What* you're gonna be is dead, unless you put that revolver away and go back where you came from."

"You just called me a yellow son of a bitch. Don't nobody call me no yellow sumbitch an' live to tell about it." As the words left his mouth the muscles in his gun hand tightened a fraction, and that was all Slocum needed to act.

He triggered off a booming shot, feeling the .44 buck in his fist. Bob Younger fired as he was falling backward, a reflex when a bullet tore through his left shoulder. Both gunshots echoed off storefronts, then the sound died. Bob fell over on his back with his pistol still clutched in his hand.

"Jesus! Damn!" Younger shouted, rocking back and forth in the dirt in the grips of sudden pain. He dropped his gun and reached for his injured shoulder, raising his head off the ground to give Slocum a look.

Slocum walked toward him. "I warned you," he said, coming to Younger's pistol, kicking it away from easy reach. "Next time somebody promises to shoot you, maybe you'll listen."

Younger's expression became a mask of hatred in spite of the pain in his arm. He stared up at Slocum. "I'll get you for this you son of a bitch," he hissed, clenching his teeth in a mixture of agony and anger.

Slocum allowed himself a mirthless grin. "You tried it once and it got you that hole in your arm. If you're stupid enough to try again, the next hole I put in you is gonna be where your nose meets up with your eyes, only you won't feel a thing. You'll hear this little cracking noise, and then all your troubles with card games will be over when you sleep the long sleep."

The young man in baggy trousers and rumpled suit-coat got to his feet, looking at Slocum. "I'm Billy Jackson, an' I'm mighty glad you came along when you did, stranger. I was travelin' west when I stopped at the Steamboat Saloon for a few drinks and a game of cards. This cowboy called me a cheat when I won a hand of poker and he tossed me out the back door, sayin' he was gonna teach me a lesson. I'm most grateful for what you did just now and I don't know how to thank you."

Slocum lowered his Colt, although he held it ready at his side, recalling what the liveryman said, that Bob Younger had a brother. "No need to say any more, Mr. Jackson, but I'd advise you to stay away from the Steamboat. I've heard it said they've got some tough customers."

Jackson dusted off his pants and picked up a derby hat near his feet. He looked to be in his early twenties, and if Slocum could tell by the cut of his clothes, a drummer by trade.

"I'd be glad to buy you a drink or two," Jackson added as he put the bowler on his head.

"No need for that either," Slocum replied. "Just keep on heading west so this loudmouth or some of his friends don't give you any more problems. This one won't be doing much harm for a few weeks, until his shoulder heals."

"I'll be leaving right away," Jackson said, offering his hand. "If you wouldn't mind my asking, what's your name, so I'll know who came to my rescue."

Slocum knew Bob Younger would remember the name if he heard it, and probably tell his brother and

Red Sloan who put a bullet in his arm. But Slocum had never been bashful about giving his identity, nor was he about to change that practice because of a risk of revenge. "John Slocum," he said, taking Jackson's palm.

Bob Younger's eyes became slits before Slocum holstered his gun and walked away.

5

He was eating a late lunch at the Capitol Cafe when a man with a star pinned to his vest entered the place. For a moment the peace officer's eyes wandered the room, until they came to rest on Slocum.

"It's something to do with the shooting," he muttered as he spooned chicken and dumplings into his mouth, watching the lawman approach his table. He was a portly fellow, big around the waist with sloping shoulders and a round face sporting a neatly trimmed handlebar mustache.

"You the feller who shot Bob Younger today?" he asked as he stopped at Slocum's table, watching him eat chicken and dumplings.

Slocum looked up, irritated by the intrusion. "I believe that was the gent's name. I shot a man in the arm who was about to put a bullet into an unarmed man. He pointed his gun at me, and I pulled the trigger. It was self-defense and there were at least two dozen witnesses."

The sheriff's eyes flickered around the room again, to see who might be listening. "I'm not here to arrest you," he said. "I already talked to some witnesses an' your story matches what they told me. I'm Sheriff John Myers." He extended his hand. "I came to offer you a deputy's job, if you're interested."

"Not interested," Slocum replied, shaking his head. "I'm just passing through town."

"Mind if I sit?" the sheriff asked, drawing back a chair without waiting for Slocum's reply.

"Suit yourself. I'm having lunch."

"I need to tell you a few things," Sheriff Myers began. "The feller you shot is a mean bastard with a gun, and he's got a brother who'll come after you for what you did. If I was in your shoes I'd leave town before Clay Younger comes lookin' for you."

"I'd planned to leave tomorrow," Slocum said around a big mouthful of dumplings.

Myers's eyebrows came together. "That could be too late, Mr. Slocum."

"I've already made my plans. I'll be pulling out some time tomorrow morning."

"I don't think you understand," Myers continued, after a second glance over his shoulder. "Those Younger boys are about as tough as they come. An' to make matters worse, they've got this *compadre* who may be the worst killer of all. His name is Lyle Sloan, an' he's from up 'round Fort Worth, the Hells Half Acre part of town. If you ain't from these parts, let me tell you for sure these boys ain't the kind to fool around with. A man with good sense would ride out of Austin before they find you, to get even for what you done to Bob."

Slocum eyed the sheriff, halting the motion of his spoon. "I never let anybody else make my travel plans, Sheriff. I aim to stay in Austin till tomorrow."

"That could be a fool's move. You don't know what you're gettin' yourself into."

He was growing tired of the sheriff's banter. "You wear the badge around here, so it's your job to protect citizens from lawless types. Isn't that what you're being paid to do?"

Myers looked away. "I'm not gettin' paid enough to go up against the likes of them. You proved you can handle yourself in a tight spot when Bob drew down on that drummer, an' that's how come I wanted to know if you'd be interested in a deputy's position. Even for a little while."

"I told you before I'm not interested," Slocum said, his voice betraying impatience. "And I'm not worried if the other brother or this Lyle Sloan comes after me to try to settle the score. I mind my own business, for the most part. But when I saw that boy lying in the street with a gun pointed at him, I took a hand in affairs that weren't really mine. It goes against my grain to see somebody get pushed. Younger was pushing the kid, so I showed him what it was like to get pushed back."

"Some of the witnesses said you were good with a gun, that you coulda killed Bob, only you didn't. Him an' his brother have been pushin' folks ever since they came to town, an' I ain't good enough with a gun to put a stop to it."

Slocum's temper cooled some. "When a man, no matter how bad or tough he thinks he is, finds himself looking down the barrel of a gun, he usually mellows some. Younger didn't think I'd have the nerve to shoot him. Now he knows how wrong he was."

Myers's shoulders drooped and he wore a downcast expression. "I tried to form-up a posse, only nobody would join. A lot of folks in this town don't seem to care if these bad actors kill each other, so long as they stay near the saloon district. One member of the city council told me it was all right with him if they thinned themselves out a bit by killin' a few of their own breed. I wired for the Texas Rangers to lend me a hand with cleanin' it up, only they sent a telegram up from San Antone sayin' they couldn't spare no men an' didn't have any plans to bring a company back to Austin right away. It's all those Indian troubles. The damn Comanch' are on the warpath west of the Leon River plumb to Palo Duro Canyon. Even the army can't stop 'em from liftin' hair, so the Rangers are tryin' to track those war parties down for the soldiers. Leaves me with no help handlin' a gang of rowdies. Makes matters worse when nobody at the Steamboat will be a witness to the killin' goin' on in there, because they're scared of retribution if they talk. Even if I had enough deputies, I couldn't get Judge Jones to charge 'em with anything because won't no witnesses say a damn word against none of that bunch. Every time there's a killin' at the Steamboat, them Youngers or Sloan claims it was self-defense and not a soul will say otherwise."

"Folks scare easy," Slocum remarked, returning to his bowl but without appetite. "Leastways some do."

"You wasn't scared, Mr. Slocum. That drummer told me your name, an' about how you never so much as blinked when you held a gun on Bob an' pulled the trigger."

Slocum put his spoon down. "Look, Sheriff, I'd like to be some help, but I'm on my way to see some old acquaintances north of here and it really isn't my problem. Maybe the Rangers will show up in a week or so." He glanced down at Myers's Peacemaker holstered on his right hip. One look at the way he carried it told Slocum the man wouldn't be much good with a gun in a contest with an experienced shootist. He wore his pistol high and its placement would make his draw too slow, too awkward. "Don't take this personal, but maybe you oughta give some thought to getting out of the lawman's profession. It don't seem to suit you."

Myers looked at his hands folded on the tabletop. "I've discovered a number of things while I've been in office," he confided quietly. "I'm no match for these hired assassins, an' I'd counted on a few good citizens to step forward when it was necessary. I've been sorely disappointed. Since this wild bunch took over the Steamboat I've been doin' a lot of thinkin' on it. Some folks already claim I couldn't get elected again after the way I backed down from those killers. But I've done decided I won't run for sheriff again, an' if things get any worse I'll hand the city council this badge an' quit."

Slocum found he'd begun to develop a bit of sympathy for the sheriff's plight, trying to keep law and order in a town where no one would join a posse to clean out a bad element. "It sounds like you've got a man-sized job on your hands," he agreed, "but I'm just passing through so I wouldn't be any help. I try to mind my own business, whenever circumstances allow."

Myers nodded and prepared to stand up. "I understand, Mr. Slocum. Didn't do no harm to ask. By all accounts you handled Bob Younger like he wasn't nothin' at all. I envy you for that. I only wish I had the know-how. I'd walk in that place an' put 'em all in wrist irons, or kill 'em deader'n fence posts if they refused to come quietly." He held out his hand to Slocum. "Pleased to make your acquaintance," he said.

Slocum shook with him before the sheriff got out of his chair. "Best of luck, Sheriff. Maybe those Rangers will show up in a little while and your problem will be solved. Even the bad boys, the worst of the lot, won't face up to a squad of Rangers. Some Rangers I've known are nearly as hell-bent on killing a man as the men they're after. Only difference is the badge."

Myers took a look at the door. "You watch yourself until you clear out of town tomorrow," he said. "My money says Clay Younger or Lyle Sloan will be gunnin' for you. You might give some serious consideration to leavin' town today, if you aim to steer clear of a bullet."

"I'll think it over," Slocum said, knowing he wouldn't. He had never run from a fight in his life and he wasn't about to be changing old habits to avoid trouble.

He found Cobbs standing outside his livery as dusk fell on the Colorado River bottom. The stablekeeper had another piece of straw in his mouth, rolling it across his tongue. He grinned when he saw Slocum walk up.

"You made quite a stir here today," he said. "Half the folks up an' down Sixth Street been talkin' about it. Tell me the straight of it, Mr. Slocum . . . did you really outdraw Bob Younger in a pistol duel?"

Slocum wagged his head—this was how stories and reputations got exaggerated. He continued toward the stud's stall. "That isn't the way it happened," he said, seeing the bay prick up its ears when it heard his voice. "Younger was holding a gun on an unarmed drummer, claiming the boy cheated him at cards. I came along just when Younger was about to shoot holes in the boy's hands, so I drew my forty-four and told Younger to holster his gun. He turned it on me instead, and when he did, I shot him through the shoulder. Wasn't much to it, actually. It sure as hell wasn't any contest to see who could pull iron first."

"That ain't the way some folks are tellin' it, mister. I was told you pulled on him an' gunned him down flat." Cobbs eyed Slocum's pistol under the tail of his frock coat. "You'd best keep lookin' behind you," he added, glancing up and down the street. "Clay an' Sloan will be lookin' for you."

"The sheriff said the same thing," Slocum replied, reaching over the stall door to rub the stud's neck. "Glad to see you're taking good care of my horse. He looks full in the flanks and that swelling is down in his pasterns."

"I rubbed him down with linament," Cobbs said, "but if I was you I wouldn't be worryin' so much about the condition of my horse. I'd be worried about my backside."

Slocum turned away from the stall. "I never worry unless I know there's something to worry about. Right now, till I find out if Clay Younger or Lyle Sloan are as mean as everybody claims, I'm gonna go about my business as usual. If they show up and care to test me, I'll oblige 'em, but until then I intend to enjoy the company of a pretty lady and a bottle of good brandy."

Cobbs looked like he couldn't quite believe it. "You've got nerves made of iron, Mr. Slocum, unless you're bluffin' with all that tough talk."

Slocum started back down the hallway of the barn. "I never bluff anybody," he replied, "not even when I'm playing poker. If I've got a hand I play it, and if it don't, I toss it in and look for another game."

Cobbs hooked his thumbs in his suspenders. "You may just find yourself wishin' you'd tossed in the cards you drew today," he said.

Slocum looked over his shoulder as he stepped into a dusky street darkening with night. "I don't reckon I'll know for sure until I meet up with Sloan or Younger, if it happens. Left up to me, I'd see the lady tonight and be on my way tomorrow morning without any fuss."

"That'll be another thing that makes 'em mad," Cobbs said to Slocum's back as he swung toward the hotel. "If

Sloan finds out you're seein' Myra, he'll be fit to be tied an' sure as hell come lookin' for you."

Slocum didn't answer the liveryman. It was pointless to argue the subject with him. Cobbs had allowed the reputations of three so-called bad men to put fear into his heart, and fear was usually any man's worst enemy.

He crossed LaVaca Street and came to Sixth, where he made a turn for the Driskell Hotel to take a hot bath and shave off his whisker stubble. As he strolled down darkening streets his eyes roamed the boardwalks, not out of fear, but from years of caution, caution that had kept him alive.

He walked up to a beautiful lady with a shawl around her shoulders, her soft brown hair tied up in ribbons. He took off his hat and bowed to her politely, saying, "Evening, ma'am."

She returned his bow with a nod, a hint of a smile, as she continued along the boardwalk.

Slocum grinned as he came to a corner of Sixth Street. "I sure do like the scenery around here," he muttered, crossing after a wagon laden with flour barrels lumbered past.

At the hotel he waved to the clerk. "Will you ask Ida Lee if she'll draw me a hot bath?" he asked, crossing the lobby to head up the stairs.

"I surely will, Mr. Slocum," the old man replied. "An' by the way, there was this real tall feller who inquired about you a while ago. He didn't give his name. He was wearin' a black suit coat with a split tail an' a black flat brim hat, an' I also did happen to notice he was wearin' a gun tied down low on his leg. He had these funny-colored gray eyes, an' when he asked 'bout you his voice sounded like he had somethin' caught in his throat, a real deep sound, if you know what I mean. I thought maybe you'd recognize him if I gave you his description."

"Not off hand," Slocum answered, starting up the steps. He was sure what the tied-down gun meant. Lyle Sloan, or Clay Younger, had made the inquiry, and now they knew where he was staying while he was in Austin.

6

His senses warned him that something was wrong as he walked slowly down the hallway to his room. He'd learned to trust the feeling during the war when it came to him, without knowing what it was that made him wary, on edge. He went up on the balls of his feet, and opened his coat so he could reach his gun while he took the key to his room from his pocket with his left hand. It was like a bad smell, when he sensed he was about to walk into a trap, and the feeling rarely ever failed him.

When he came quietly to the door of his room he hesitated and listened closely. The hallway was dark. Nothing stirred behind his door and still he had a gnawing feeling someone was there.

Slocum drew his Colt and gently pushed the key into the lock as his muscles tensed, ready for action. He heard the tumblers click, and he knew anyone waiting inside would also hear them and know he was about to enter the room. He took a deep breath, then gave the doorknob a twist, as prepared as he could be for trouble on the other side.

The door swung soundlessly inward. Slocum's eyes swept the room, what he could see of it standing outside, examining every shadow for a shape that did not belong. For a few silent seconds he stood there, trigger finger poised, swinging his gun barrel back and forth. Once, he thought he heard someone breathing, a single breath, although he couldn't be sure of the sound, or exactly where it came from. If someone was waiting for him here, looking for revenge for the wound he inflicted on Bob Younger, would he use a gun? Or something quieter? A knife. Maybe a club.

When nothing moved, and when he heard no more sounds, he took a cautious step across the threshold, wary of someone hiding behind the door, preparing himself for it as best he could. His attention was directed toward a spot behind the door and thus he was not fully ready when a dark figure came lunging at him from the other side of the room.

Slocum ducked and turned his gun, but not before a clubbing blow crashed against his left ear. He staggered and fell, still clinging to his pistol as he landed on his chest beside the bed. His head reeled, the sensation of spinning at dizzying speed. A thousand flashing lights winked before his eyes, fireflies across his field of vision. He heard himself groan, an involuntary cry of pain and surprise.

"You bastard!" someone snapped. A boot toe went thudding into his ribs, driving all the air from his lungs.

Slocum tried to roll over, and when he made the attempt, a second kick caught him in the jaw, slamming him to the floor on his back.

"I'll teach you to point a goddamn gun at my brother, you son of a bitch!" The voice was hoarse, full of menace and pent-up rage.

Slocum curled into a ball as white-hot pain raced

across his ribcage and down his jawbone to his neck where the boot found its mark, while he struggled to remain conscious from the first blow to his head—he knew his life hung in the balance and yet he had no way to defend himself, rendered almost senseless by so many vicious kicks and whatever had struck his skull the moment he entered the room. Despite the fog swirling around in his brain he knew by what was said that his attacker was Clay Younger, and he also understood that unless he found the strength to use his gun, he was destined for a terrible beating, or death at the hands of Bob's enraged brother.

He felt a tremendous weight land on his wrist, pinning his gun hand and gun to the floor, a heavy foot that sent waves of pain from his wrist to his fingertips, forcing his grip on the Colt to relax—it slipped from his grasp, thudding softly on a floor of polished boards.

"I oughta kill you now!" his attacker hissed, "only I promised my brother I'd make you hurt, make you bleed like you done to him!"

Slocum shook his head to clear it, just in time to catch a glimpse of a dark object resembling a tree limb sweeping toward his face. He felt something crack against the top of his skull and suddenly, everything went black.

He knew it was a dream, a dream from the war when it seemed almost every day would be his last. Sergeant John Slocum commanded Confederate sharpshooters at Little Round Top and it was there where he found his younger brother, Lieutenant Robert Slocum, dead on the battlefield after Pickett's charge. He knelt beside Robert and stared into his glazed eyes with so much sorrow in his heart that he couldn't cry . . . his feelings were beyond tears right then. Coal oil lanterns bobbed across the battlefield as Confederate soldiers searched for the living among the dead during the night. It seemed added punishment that he would be the one to find Robert, to see his bullet-torn body lying in a patch of bloody grass staring blankly at a night sky full of stars. Slocum had taken his Dance .44 revolver from its holster as a precaution against Union sharpshooters, and when he found Robert's corpse, he tossed his pistol aside, a symbolic gesture that somehow, he was finished with this war in his heart and soul. There would be more fighting, but now a part of him would rest in a grave with his brother for the rest of his life. He would be changed from that moment on.

He gathered Robert into his arms and staggered under his weight, stumbling back toward Confederate lines with another kind of weight in his heart. His brother's arms and legs hung limply and the scent of Robert's blood filled his nostrils, nostrils burned during the battle by smoking gunpowder and the stench of death all around him.

Slocum felt tears roll down his cheeks and yet he was not aware of his crying, soft sobbing sounds coming from deep in his chest.

"Who goes there?" a harsh voice demanded from the darkness.

Slocum knew that voice. "It's me, Wayland. I found Robert."

A slender soldier emerged from the darker shadow beneath a tree, a musket in his hands. "Is he . . . alive?"

Slocum's throat was so tight he could not answer, stumbling onward blindly with tears coursing down his face.

"Oh no," Corporal Burke whispered, dropping his musket before he trotted down a grassy hillside to Slocum's side. "I ain't exactly sure what to say, John—"

"Nothing to be said," Slocum replied, as Wayland

lifted Robert's legs to assist with carrying him. "Too late for any words now. Maybe a little prayin' tomorrow morning after I dig his grave."

"I'm awful sorry," Wayland told him quietly as they went up the hill with Robert's corpse between them, dark blood leaking from Robert's wounds, dribbling on their boots. "I reckon that's about all there is to say."

They carried the body to a row of hospital tents, and passed the tents to an open field where hundreds of corpses lay, awaiting burial.

"I'll inform General Pickett," Slocum said, walking toward a grassy spot beneath an oak tree. "Right now, I think I'd like to be alone with my brother for a spell."

"But he's dead," Wayland had said, as they gently placed the body at the foot of the tree. "Maybe it wouldn't be the best thing to stay with him, John. It'll keep remindin' you of what happened."

Slocum turned angrily, until he collected himself so harsh words wouldn't be directed to his friend. "I'm well aware of what happened, Wayland. Just leave me be for a little while. I've got some thinking to do."

Wayland wiped blood off his palms. "Sorry, John. I only figured stayin' with him might make things worse. I'll tell the first soldier from Stonewall Jackson's divisions I see that you are here with your brother's body."

"I'd be obliged," Slocum said, sitting in the grass beside Robert, fighting back more tears when a tidal wave of memories from their childhood threatened to overwhelm him. "Just tell whoever you see that I'll report first thing in the morning."

Wayland turned to leave, then he stopped. "It's gonna sound dumb, me sayin' this, but at least you're still alive. A lot of good men died out there today, an' in spite of what fate did to your brother, I'm sure as hell glad you made it through without no holes in your hide."

Slocum nodded, his jaw clamped. "I'm real glad you made it too, Wayland. It's hard to figure, how some make it and some don't stand a chance. Robert, he was always too damn brave for his own good. Back when we were kids he'd fight the toughest boys in school, even when he knew he couldn't whip 'em. I tried to tell him it didn't make sense to take an ass whippin' for no reason other than to prove a point, that he wasn't scared of nobody on this earth. He didn't listen back then. And it don't appear he did much listening to me durin' this war."

"Chargin' up that hill were his orders, John," Wayland reminded.

"Yeah. He could follow orders, too. General Pickett told him one time that he was a hell of a good soldier. It don't seem fair, that this is what happens to good soldiers. But there's a whole battlefield full of 'em out there tonight who fought brave and hard before a minnieball struck 'em down."

"This whole damn war don't make no sense to me, John. We ain't got any slaves, so why the hell are we doin' all the dyin' for them that does?"

"It isn't just about slavery," Slocum replied in a quiet voice. "It's more complicated than that. Some rich bastards in Washington wanted to tell folks in the South how to live, that we had to live by their rules. A southern state couldn't make up its own mind about how to run things, they said. Abe Lincoln told the South to knuckle under, and that just ain't our style. The way my pa explained it, we didn't have any choice but to fight."

Wayland looked over his shoulder, toward the carnage of a night-blackened battlefield. "Sure were a lot of men killed here today over an idea," he said.

Slocum gently folded Robert's arms across his chest, then he left his right palm resting on his brother's hands.

"Damn rotten luck," he whispered, talking to himself now.

"I'll bring you somethin' to eat," Wayland promised as he turned away.

"No need of that," Slocum replied softly. "Got no appetite. But thanks for the offer anyway."

"I'll see if I can find some corn whiskey. Tommy Strunk had a dash in his canteen this mornin'. Maybe a little whiskey would help."

Slocum closed his eyes a moment. "I sure as hell wouldn't turn no whiskey down tonight," he said later, when more memories of Robert flooded his brain, of Calhoun County in Georgia, and Robert's love of good horses, his expert horsemanship, how much he liked to fish in the creeks crossing their five-hundred acre farm. They had worked side by side almost since they were old enough to walk, helping their pa till the soil, and while Robert was a bit shorter, he had the same black hair and green eyes as his older brother, eyes that caught the notice of young girls and later, girls in the full flower of womanhood. He and Robert had been so close all their lives: meeting girls, fishing and hunting and riding horses, working the land, putting up hay in the spring and summer, tending to their livestock. There were times when it seemed they could read each other's thoughts. And now that was ended, ended by a ball of molten lead fired by a Yankee who probably never knew his bullet struck down a man, for in the hail of gunfire at Gettysburg no one could be sure who felled an enemy or who missed. If only the musket balls could have missed Robert Slocum . . .

"Be back quick as I can," Wayland said. "I imagine whiskey is gonna be in short supply, after today. A man who don't want a drink after this fight ain't right in the head."

Slocum wasn't listening, still caught up in recollections of his dead brother. He remembered the pocket watch their father had given Robert and, in a trancelike state, Slocum put his hand in Robert's pockets until he found the watch, knowing what he had to do. It had to be sent back home, along with the grim message telling of Robert's death.

He heard Wayland's footsteps moving away into the night while he removed the watch and held it in his palm. Then he looked at his brother's lifeless face in light from the stars. "Sorry, Bobby boy," he whispered, gently closing his fingers around the timepiece. "You were always lucky with horses, and with women. I reckon your luck just ran out today. It'll break Ma's heart when I send this watch home without you. They'll know, even before they read the letter, what this means."

He closed his eyes, until he heard footfalls coming from another direction. Looking up, he found a Confederate captain from Jackson's Brigades walking toward him, Captain Clyde Stark of the Sixth Virginia Cavalry.

Captain Stark stopped a few feet away. "What are you doin' just sittin' there, Sergeant?" Stark asked harshly.

Slocum swallowed. "Spendin' a few minutes with my brother, Cap'n, before we bury him."

The captain's tone changed, softening. "Sorry, son. Carry on. We'll be buryin' a hell of a lot of good men come sunrise."

Slocum tried to keep his voice from breaking when he said, "I sure do wish one of 'em hadn't been Lieutenant Robert Slocum, sir."

7

He drifted in and out of consciousness, only dimly aware
of his surroundings when he awakened for brief periods.
He was in a room, lying on a bed, but his eyes would
not focus and he couldn't tell where he was. Then he
would slide back into a deep slumber full of troubling
dreams, vaporous images dancing before him like tiny
swirls of mist rising from a lake or a spring-fed stream
in wintertime. He saw faces detached from bodies float-
ing at the edge of a gray fog, and he felt cold. At times
he heard distant, unfamiliar voices, however for the most
part he found himself surrounded by absolute silence.

The dreams were often frightening things, glimpses of
his past, the faces of men he'd killed, or his brother's
face, or those of his ma and pa. There were faces he
didn't recognize, and every now and then he was certain
someone was talking to him even though the words .
sounded like jibberish, unrecognizable as language he
understood. The sensation of feeling cold remained with
him throughout—he felt himself shivering.

Time lost all meaning, for it seemed he was lost in a
world of dreams forever. Was he dead? he wondered.

Was this what the afterlife was like? He was never a religious man, yet he believed in a Creator, having spent a good many years in church back in Georgia when he was a boy, at his parent's insistence. Could he truly be dead now, experiencing what the Bible called hell? It was indeed a terrifying place, wherever he was. And no matter where his strange dreams took him, Robert was always there and Slocum could see his face. But when he tried to call out to his brother, he discovered he had no voice, only the urge to speak to his long-dead sibling even though he was unable to make a sound.

"Swallow this, Mr. Slocum," a faraway voice said.

He opened his eyes. A gray-bearded man stood over him with a spoon.

"Take this medicine," the stranger said. "It's laudanum an' it'll help ease the pain."

"Where am I?" he asked feebly, blinking.

"City Hospital," the man replied. "I'm Doc Hardin. You got some mighty serious injuries, but I think you'll live. Bumps all over your head where they struck you are the worst."

"It was just one man," Slocum remembered. "I'm pretty sure his name is Clay Younger. I had a little run-in with his brother today."

The doctor grunted. "That was three days ago. I treated Bob for a bullet wound. The slug passed through clean, so he'll mend pretty quick. You've been asleep for quite a spell."

"Three days?" Slocum couldn't believe he'd been unconscious for so long.

"Swallow," Dr. Hardin said, forcing the spoon between Slocum's lips. "You took one hell of a beatin', mister. You can count yourself lucky to be alive."

He swallowed bitter liquid as his thoughts began to

clear. "I saw him lunge for me with a club of some kind. Then he kicked me several times before I blacked out. That's about all I can remember right now. I heard him say I'd be sorry for aiming a gun at his brother, so I figure it had to be Clay."

Hardin nodded and put down his spoon. "This whole town is scared of that crowd. They're a bunch of bad characters. I've been told they killed five men since they got here, an' busted up a few more. We've got a sheriff who won't face up to 'em an' they've had a free hand over in the saloon district, in particular at the Steamboat Saloon."

"So I'd heard," Slocum remarked. He attempted to lift his head and fell back, his brain swimming.

"It's too early for that, Mr. Slocum," Hardin warned. "I'd guess you're lookin' at a few days in bed, maybe a week."

"I can't stay that long," Slocum said. "I'm on my way up to McLennan County to see an old friend."

"You won't be sittin' a saddle for quite a spell either," the doctor said. "You've got some badly bruised ribs an' those knots on your head will interfere with your balance a while. A brain bleeds just like any other part of a human body. You've got some blood on your brain. Some was leakin' out your ears when they brought you in."

Slocum stirred beneath a bedsheet, testing the movement of his legs and arms. "I can make it," he promised. "It'll take a minute or two for me to get my head clear."

Hardin frowned, putting a cork in a purple bottle at Slocum's bedside. "You may be tough, Mr. Slocum, but you ain't that tough. Nobody is. When a man gets the hell beaten outta him like you did, his body requires time to heal proper. You won't be no exception."

He traced a fingertip across his ribs, wincing when he

felt a stab of pain. Then he touched the bumps on his head one at a time before he dropped his hand on the mattress beside him. As his consciousness fully returned, so did his anger. "Where's my gun?" he asked, glancing around the hospital room. "Soon as I can get my boots and clothes on I'm gonna pay a call on Mr. Clay Younger."

The doctor wagged his head. "That wouldn't be smart, son. Look what he already did to you—"

"He was waiting for me in a dark room. He jumped me. I'll make damn sure things are different when I meet up with him again and that's a promise."

"I've seen him," Hardin said. "He's big an' tough an' he's just about the last man on earth I'd go lookin' for. He's good with a gun, too."

Slocum's teeth came together. He bit down hard when he said, "He'd better be good, because I aim to test him. It sticks in my craw when somebody bushwhacks me. Younger pushed me a little too hard this time, and he's gonna pay."

Hardin turned away from Slocum's bed. "That's mighty strong talk. You'd best be able to back it up if you're crazy enough to go lookin' for him."

Slocum gave Dr. Hardin a hard stare. "I've hardly ever made a promise I didn't keep, Doc, and I'm not about to develop a new set of habits now. Leave me a bottle of that painkiller. I'll get dressed as soon as I'm able and then I'll pay your bill."

The doctor seemed amused. "You'll never make it across the room, Mr. Slocum, not in your condition. But it appears you're dead-set on tryin'. Your clothes an' your pistols are in that wardrobe closet in the corner, if you make it that far. I'm of the opinion you won't be able to get out of this bed, much less do any walkin' around."

Slocum looked up at the ceiling, certain that his pain would intensify when he moved around and got dressed. "I've been hurt a few times worse'n this, Doc. I'll manage. I intend to tell Sheriff Myers about what happened, then I'm going down to the Steamboat as soon as I'm able."

Hardin hesitated at the door to Slocum's room. "Sheriff Myers came by, inquirin' about you . . . about your condition. He said important business would take him out of town for a few days an' to tell you he warned you ahead of time that somethin' like this would happen." The doctor shook his head again. "We've got no law in this town. Nobody wanted the job in the first place. Some folks say we'd be better off with nobody than with what we've got. John Myers ain't a bad feller, he just sure as hell ain't a lawman."

Slocum remembered his conversation with Myers at the cafe. "He says he can't raise a posse. Enough armed men could run the Youngers and Lyle Sloan out of town or put 'em into a jail cell."

Hardin scratched absently through his beard, appearing to be deep in thought a moment. "That's the funny thing about Austin, if you ask me. It's got a reputation as a bad place because folks look the other way when there's a problem. I've watched it happen over the years. It could be said about this city it's full to the brim with cowards who like to complain. As soon as there's any violence, everybody runs an' hides, like they think it'll go away by itself."

Slocum raised his head, this time more slowly, getting used to the swimming sensation as best he could as the laudanum began to take effect. "Under some conditions, there's only one way to establish law and order in a town. The law of the gun. Every now and then it's necessary to kill off a few of the bad types as a lesson to the others."

Hardin watched Slocum carefully as he eased himself up on his elbows.

"Do you intend to try to kill Clay Younger?" he asked, and by the tone of it he sounded like he didn't believe it was possible.

Slocum's arms were trembling and he required a moment before he found the strength to answer. "I plan to teach Younger some manners, Doc, same as I did his brother. And if this Lyle Sloan gets in the way, he'll get the same schoolin'."

The doctor watched Slocum bring his legs gingerly off one side of the bed. "Maybe you are just tough enough to do it," he said. "I'd have made a big wager that you couldn't get those feet on the floor just now. Take it easy, if you want my advice on it. Give yourself a little time."

"I haven't got the time," Slocum replied, gritting his teeth so tightly his jaw muscles hurt.

"I'd think about it," Hardin said, "before I challenged men like them. Even if you are as tough as you think you are, you'd better be at your best before you take them on in a gunfight."

Slocum's ribcage was throbbing and his head felt like it would explode. He reached for the footboard of the bed to steady himself with his right hand, and as he did a twinge of sharp pain reminded him of Younger's boot landing on his wrist. "I can make it," he told the doctor, only now he was beginning to have serious doubts— with a crippled gun hand he would be at a big disadvantage.

"You may just be askin' to get yourself killed, Mr. Slocum. I suggest a couple of days of rest. Let the healin' do its work a while longer."

"I'll see if I can stand up." Gripping the footboard, he leaned forward and tried to push himself to his feet. "Damn that hurts," he groaned, swaying when he straightened his knees, beads of sweat popping out on his forehead. "It even hurts like hell to breathe."

"Take my advice. Wait a few days."

He eyed the wardrobe closet, wondering now if the doctor could be right. His limbs were trembling and flashes of pain raced down his arms, across his chest while his skull was hammering.

"The laudanum will make your reflexes slow," Hardin added in a somber tone, "and you have some abrasions on your right wrist. If you're right-handed, your flexibility will be impaired. You will experience problems drawin' and usin' a gun."

Slocum took a tentative step toward the closet without the footboard to aid him with balance. His skin felt clammy now from head to toe. "I haven't got the strength to pull my boots on," he said, staggering, almost falling.

Dr. Hardin hurried over to steady him by his elbow. "Lie back down," he said gently. "You can't make it down the stairs, much less face the man who did this to you."

"I have to try," Slocum protested, testing his weight with his knees locked before he took another step.

"Don't be a fool. Lie down until some of your strength returns."

His legs were trembling violently and the room began to spin in lazy circles. "Help me with my boots, Doc. If you can help me get 'em on I'll do the rest—"

Hardin's expression grew stern. "I won't help a man get himself killed. If you can't dress yourself you sure as hell can't handle a gun."

A blanket of black fog crept into the edges of Slocum's vision. Stars twinkled before his eyes in a place where there could be no stars. "Help . . . me," he moaned as he felt his knees buckle.

"Nurse Collins!" Hardin shouted into the hall. "Come here quickly!"

The doctor was too small and frail to keep Slocum from going to the floor on his rump, causing more blinding chains of pain to course through him. The room was spinning at a faster pace now, making him queasy.

He saw a woman in a blue uniform wearing a white nurse's cap hurry into the room. "What on earth?" she gasped, coming to his side.

"He tried to leave," Hardin said. "Help me lift him back into bed. He's big, and very muscular, so he's heavier than most men."

"Yes doctor," the nurse replied, kneeling down.

"He has badly damaged ribs, so be careful when we lift him by the arms," the doctor added, taking Slocum's left arm while Nurse Collins took his right. "We'll try to pick him up gently if we can."

He felt himself being hoisted off the floor, and was helpless to assist them in his weakened condition. They got him to the edge of the mattress with great difficulty, then his head was lowered to the pillow.

His last moment of consciousness slipped away as he heard Dr. Hardin say to the nurse, "Some men are too tough for their own good . . ."

8

He was limping when he came down the hospital steps, not due to leg injuries, rather from a dull ache in his ribs on the left side of his body where Clay Younger's boot toe had done the most damage. Yesterday, when he fell to the floor trying to get to a wardrobe where his clothes and guns were stored, the pain simply was too much for him. He remembered collapsing on the floor and not much else until this morning when a combination of laudanum and bed rest allowed him to move without blacking out again. He found his poke emptied when he put on his pants this afternoon, a reasonable guess that Younger had robbed him after the beating. A wire to his bank in Denver would be enough to get him money from an Austin bank until funds were shipped by rail. He had a twenty dollar banknote sewn inside the lining of his split-tail coat and a ten dollar gold piece hidden in his right boot, thus he would be able to pay for the hotel room and stabling his horse, besides a few other necessities. But a far more pressing bit of unfinished business would precede his telegram requesting cash. Clay Younger had a debt to pay, and Slocum owed an explanation to Myra Reed as to the reason why he failed to pick her up in a rented carriage that night.

"Maybe she already knows," he mumbled, taking each step in slow order to keep his ribs from hurting. "She kept company with Lyle Sloan, so they say."

Dr. Hardin had been right about one thing, that he was in no shape to ride a horse. Each step he took pained his ribs so badly it would be impossible to take the jolting of a horse's gait without subjecting himself to blinding agony. It was clear he'd be resting up in Austin for a spell, until he was well enough to travel.

Limping toward the Driskell Hotel, he pondered the wisdom of going after Younger so soon. It was true, what the doctor said, that the wrist of his gun hand remained swollen and painful, with a stiffness he hadn't noticed until now.

"Maybe I oughta wait a couple of days," he muttered, his face twisted in a grimace. But it was his deep anger that kept him thinking otherwise as he crossed a side street to Fifth Street. It was payback time for Younger, yet Slocum had to wonder if he could manage it in his condition.

He was sweating despite cool fall weather when he reached the Driskell's front steps. Using a handrail, he climbed them and went inside.

"Howdy, Mr. Slocum," the desk clerk said when he saw him come close to the counter. "Glad to see you're okay. I had you figured for dead when they hauled you outta here. My wife heard the disturbance upstairs, all that bangin' around, an' she's the one who called me to see what it was. You lost a lot of blood that night. I had Darlene clean it up an' make the bed. Your gear is right where it was—didn't nobody touch nothin'. The guy who done it must have gone down the back stairs. Never saw who it was."

Slocum guessed otherwise, but he said nothing. "I'll pay up my bill in maybe a day or two more. I'll wire Denver for more money, but I've got enough to cover my room and a few expenses."

"No need to worry," the old man replied, watching Slocum through his thick lenses. "I knowed you was a gentleman soon as you registerd. By the way, a woman asked about you yesterday. Pretty young thing, too. She said her name was Myra, an' that she wondered what came of you. I told her what took place. She said she understood, but her face sure did change colors a bit. Got as pale as a ghost, she did, when I told her about the beatin' you took upstairs."

"I'm grateful you explained it. I'll rent a buggy and go to see her tonight to make my apologies." He took the banknote from his coat lining and laid it on the counter.

The clerk counted out his change with a tiny tremor in his fingers. Slocum wondered if his nervousness was a result of knowing Clay Younger had administered the beating, after Lyle Sloan made the inquiry concerning the hotel where he was staying.

"You stay as long as you like, Mr. Slocum," the clerk said when a stack of smaller bills had been counted. "Now if you're worried about that same feller comin' back, I can give you a different room."

"No thanks," he replied, pocketing his change. "I like the view I've got. As to the part about that gent coming back, I'd like that, too. He won't find it quite so easy to jump me the next time."

Slocum turned and started upstairs to his room, thinking about Myra now. Seeing Myra again, in spite of his bad injuries, was another reason to wait before he went looking for Younger to square accounts.

● ● ●

She looked prettier than ever in a dark red velvet skirt and frilly blouse when she came over to his table at the Cattleman's Club. The place was almost empty, for it was early.

"I heard about what happened," she said quietly, looking over her shoulder at the bartender. "I heard the story from a gentleman friend of mine. He told me you wounded a man behind the Steamboat, and that someone made you pay for it with an awful beating. I'm so very sorry."

"That gentleman friend wouldn't happen to be Lyle Sloan?" he asked.

"Well, yes, but as I told you before, it's nothing permanent and we only see each other occasionally. I'm quite sure he had nothing to do with what happened to you, although he does have a rather bad reputation. Some people say he's a gunfighter, but he's always a gentleman with me."

"He wasn't the one who jumped me," Slocum told her. "I came by to apologize for not being here to escort you home the other evening. I suppose you know why I wasn't able to come."

She nodded. "Lyle told me, and he also said that if you did not die as a result of your injuries, you'd be leaving town as soon as you could. I asked at the hotel, and that's when I was told you were in the hospital. I suppose I should have come to see you after you woke up. A nurse told me you were unconscious when I went over there to see how you were."

"It was thoughtful of you to come," he said, giving her a wink. "If you're willing, I'd like to see you again tonight, if you feel the same way."

"I do," she breathed, a flush entering her cheeks. "It was a most memorable evening, the time I spent with you. You can be the nicest man . . ."

"I'll call for you in a carriage around midnight," he said, "although I must admit that I have some very sore ribs."

She smiled. "I have a remedy for sore ribs," she whispered in a tiny voice. "All you have to do is lie down on your back and I'll do the rest. Don't rent a carriage. I can walk over to the Driskell after we close. Just remember to have more of that delicious cognac."

"Consider it done," he agreed. "And now, if you'll bring me a shot or two of your best bourbon, I'll spend an hour or so here tonight, seeing as you're not all that busy yet."

Myra nodded. "I'll bring the bottle. You can pour as many as you like."

"And a good cigar. Rum-soaked, if you have them."

She curtsied politely and went to the bar. Slocum wondered what her special treatment for sore ribs might be. She said all he had to do was lie on his back.

With the lanturn in his room turned down to a mere pinpoint of light, Myra began to undress standing beside his bed. After three glasses of cognac her eyes had a wickedly wonderful gleam, a gleam that began when she undressed him first, leaving him on the mattress completely naked. She'd noticed him wincing when she unbuttoned his shirt and said, "Don't worry. I know just what to do. Take another swallow of laudanum and just lie still until I get my clothes off."

As she untied the front of her corset his erection pulsed upward, jerking away from his left leg in a series of twitches, keeping time with the beating of his heart.

Myra watched his cock lengthen and thicken with a look of pure fascination, tugging her undergarments down to her ankles, stepping out of them gracefully without once taking her eyes off his enlarging member.

"I do believe that's the biggest cock in the entire world," she sighed. "I was sore for several days after you . . . put it all inside me. This time, I'll be in control by straddling you, so you can't hurt me like you did before."

"I didn't mean to hurt you," he said, watching her pendulous breasts sway when they were free of restraint. Her pink nipples had already begun to harden, twisting into little bud-shaped points. The soft golden hair swirling around her mound caught lamp light, sparkling like dew.

Her smile widened as she approached the bed. "I know you didn't," she said huskily, eyeing his cock. "I wanted you to hurt me because it doesn't really hurt until later, the next day."

"Sorry," he told her. The shaft of his cock turned to iron. His ribs hurt some, but it was easy to forget the pain looking at a beautiful naked woman like Myra.

She knelt on the edge of the mattress and swung an ivory-smooth thigh across him very slowly, being careful not to touch him as she did it. "Just lie real still, my darling John, and I'll do everything," she whispered, lowering her glistening wet cunt slightly until it touched the tip of his member.

Using her fingers, she parted the lips of her pussy and put his cock between them, her eyes glowing now with anticipation and desire. "Oh John," she sighed. "I want you so badly and I know it'll hurt me. I can't help myself. I hope you won't think any less of me for being so forward."

"I'm very fond of a woman who can be aggressive at certain times, the right times."

"It must make me seem like a wanton slut who can't control herself," she gasped. "That's not true, not until I met you. I wish I knew what it was that makes you so different. It's not just the size of your cock . . ." She pressed downward gently and let out a sigh, closing her eyes briefly when his thickness was halted by the muscles inside her.

She started to tremble, her legs quivering with pleasure as she pushed his shaft deeper into her cunt. He could feel how wet she was, slick with juices dribbling down his member to his balls with a warmth of their own.

"Oh, that feels good," she sighed, beginning an involuntary, gentle thrusting of her groin.

Even with aching ribs he rose to meet her thrusts, ignoring the pain. His testicles drew up between his thighs in a plum-colored scrotum jiggling gently against the crack of his ass when he moved. Her juices flowed more freely now, soaking his pubic hairs, running down to the bedsheet.

"It feels wonderful," he said. "Hardly any pain at all." He reached for her breasts and held them fast, placing each of her nipples between his fingers, feeling their hardness, and the heat of warm, soft skin surrounding her knotted rosebuds.

She suddenly drove more of his cock into her cunt until the resistance was too much for her to bear, then she rocked up and down, sliding his shaft in and out, an action that made a soft sucking sound.

Now her eyes were firmly closed. "I can't take all of it," she protested, at the same time working his shaft a fraction of an inch deeper with each thrust. Her limbs shook and her breathing was much quicker.

"Take your time," he whispered, kneading her milky breasts with his fingers.

"It just won't go," she argued again, the same complaint she made when they first made love.

"You're in too big a hurry. You'll open wider. I promise you will."

"But then it really hurts—"

When his fingers tightened around her nipples she let out a moan of intensifying pleasure. "Oh dear," she whispered, forcing a bit more of his cock into her depths.

The moist heat encircling his member became a fire, and now her downward thrusting quickened.

"It's hurting me," she whimpered, while she let more of her weight down on him with every thrust.

Bedsprings started to squeak. His ribs hurt more and yet he thought of them less as Myra continued to bury another half inch of his prick inside her.

He arched his back, grimacing, when a tingling in his balls warned that the time had arrived for him to explode. "Just a little deeper," he said between clenched teeth. "I'm gonna come any minute now. I can't hold it back much longer. Let yourself go."

The rhythm of her grinding loins increased while she took much deeper, quicker breaths. "I'm coming, too, my darling. I can't wait."

She lowered herself fully, and in one powerful move she drove his cock into her all the way to the hilt. She let out a quiet cry and continued slamming her juicy cunt against the base of his swollen member until they both stiffened, straining, as his come spewed into the deepest recesses of her womb.

"Now!" she cried, slumping forward, shaking.

"That's my girl, Myra," Slocum told her, pulling her down on his chest. "When you get off you *really* do a good job of it. I can't say as I've ever known a woman any better at it."

9

Sometime during the night, as Myra lay sleeping soundly beside him, he awakened with a start, thinking he heard a noise coming along the hallway, quiet footsteps made by someone who didn't want to be heard.

He pushed himself to a sitting position, being careful to avoid too much movement in his ribcage and threw back the sheet to reach for his Colt .44 on a nightstand beside the lantern, flinching when, despite all his caution, the pain in his ribs became a fiery jolt spreading across his stomach and abdomen, even his spine.

Very slowly, he lowered his feet to the floor and crept over to the door. Pressing his ear to the wood, he listened closely as the footfalls came nearer.

"Welcome back, Mr. Younger," he whispered softly. "This time I'm gonna put a little hurt on you."

Suddenly, the noises stopped.

"Come on, Younger," he breathed, rage swelling in his chest at the thought that Younger would make another attempt on his life. Slocum was tired of pussyfooting around. This time, he would kill whoever came after him and explain it to a judge when the sheriff charged him with murder—if Myers had the nerve to do such a thing in the first place, which Slocum doubted. Myers would be as happy to be rid of the Youngers or Lyle Sloan as anyone in Austin.

A little closer, Slocum thought, tightening his grip on the gun. What the hell was the sneaky bastard waiting for?

The rustle of fabric beyond the door. Or was it the quiet movement of a gun being pulled from oiled leather?

Slocum reached for his door key inserted in the lock from the inside. He turned the key as quietly as he could to keep tumblers from making noise. Trigger finger curled around cold iron, he twisted the knob slowly, took a deep breath and jerked the door open, aiming his gun into the hall, fully prepared to kill whoever was standing there. What he saw made him freeze a fraction of a second before he pulled the trigger.

In soft light from wall-mounted oil lamps, a boy in knee-length britches stood with his slouch cap in his hands, his eyes rounded with fear and surprise when he found himself staring into the barrel of Slocum's .44.

"Don't shoot, Mr. Slocum," the youth pleaded, taking a half step backward, raising his hands. "I only came to warn you. I clean spittoons down at the Steamboat at night, an' I think I heard somethin' you might oughta hear."

Slocum sighed and lowered his Colt. "What's that, son? And don't ever sneak up on me again or I'm liable to make a mistake the next time and put a hole plumb through you."

"Sorry, sir, but I heard these men talkin' 'bout what they aim to do to you."

Slocum detected a noise behind him.

"What is it, John?" Myra asked sleepily. "I heard

voices and your side of the bed was empty—"

He spoke to her over his shoulder. "It's nothing. Go back to sleep. A kid brought me a message."

"What kind of message?" she continued, rubbing her eyes.

"It's nothing. Go back to sleep." He walked out in the hallway and closed the door behind him, looking down at the boy before he asked, "Who were these men?" He was sure he already knew.

"Them Younger brothers, an' Mr. Sloan. They said they aimed to put you in a six-foot hole tonight. They's drinkin' real hard, an' some of it may be drunk talk. But I wouldn't count on it, so I came over to where they said you was stayin', just to warn you about what they said. I work for old man Cobbs down at the livery after school. He said you was a real nice man, an' that if anybody stood a chance of gettin' this town rid of them Youngers an' Sloan, it was you, because you know your way 'round a gun. He told me you was the one who plugged Bob the other day."

"Thanks for the warning. Let me give you something for your time and trouble." Slocum opened the door and went over to the nightstand, taking a few coins from the tabletop. He gave the boy a five-cent piece and two pennies. "Buy yourself some candy canes or a licorice whip," he said, handing over the money. "I'll be ready for those owlhoots if they show up. Now, you'd better clear out of here if there's gonna be trouble."

"Yessir, an' thanks for this spendin' money. Mr. Cobbs sure do like that bay racin' stud of yours, an' I like him even better. Best-made horse I ever saw. Never saw one no better'n him."

"He's a Thoroughbred, from back east. Go home, son. If what you say is true there's liable to be some shooting here before sunrise."

"It's the honest truth, mister. I heard what they said with my own two ears." He wheeled around and ran back down the hall with his cap in one hand, Slocum's coins in the other.

Slocum listened to the kid's footsteps going down the stairs for a moment, then he shut the door and locked it.

"What was that all about?" Myra asked, still sounding like she was half asleep.

"A kid who works over at the Steamboat overheard some conversation. Clay Younger, or Lyle Sloan, may make a try at getting even with me for wounding Bob. The boy said they made mention of putting me in a grave. You've got to get out of here . . . I wouldn't want anything to happen to you."

"They mean to kill you?" she asked, flipping back the sheet, her melon-sized breasts swaying gently against her ribcage as she stood up. "I don't believe it. Lyle has always been a perfect gentleman around me. I don't believe those rumors about him being a killer."

"Get dressed, Myra," Slocum said, putting his gun down to pull on his pants, grimacing when he bent down for his stovepipe boots. He heard the girl rustling fabric as she began dressing. In light from the moon and stars pouring through a window near the bed he saw her wriggling into her corset.

"Lyle wouldn't do something like that," she said again. "I just know he wouldn't. It must be Clay who said it."

"I'm not willing to take a chance. I've got to get you out of here. Sorry, but I'm only thinking of your safety, just in case what the kid overheard is true. I'll send for a carriage as soon as we get downstairs to the lobby."

"That's okay. I can walk. I walk to work and back home almost every night anyway. It isn't all that far."

Slocum stood up and eased each arm into the sleeves of his shirt. "A gentleman never allows a lady to walk home alone, Miss Reed. Tonight won't be an exception. Follow me down the stairs and be sure to stay back a little until I make sure the lobby is empty. Clay, or your gentleman friend Mr. Sloan, may already be here at the hotel getting ready to make their play."

"Lyle wouldn't allow any harm to come to me and I'm quite sure of that," she said, coming over to him, looking into his eyes in the darkness.

He wouldn't tell her about other men he knew who were like Sloan, hired guns who had no loyalty, no respect for human life, no scruples. If Younger or Sloan wanted to get at Slocum badly enough they wouldn't worry about a woman who happened to get in the way.

He strapped on his gunbelt and tucked his bellygun inside his shirtfront. "Let's go. I'll make sure the hall is clear before we head for the stairs. Stay back. If I yell for you to get down, lie flat on the floor. There'll be less likelihood a stray bullet might catch you that way. These walls are mighty damn thin."

Slocum crossed over to the door with his .44 clamped in his right fist, twisting the knob as quietly as he could before he peered into the hallway. A moment later he stuck his head out to look both ways, finding no cause for alarm, no sounds or shadows that might be a killer lurking in the half dark where circles of light from the lamps ended.

"Follow me," he whispered, creeping out of the room with his gun leveled in front of him. "Stay back a little—"

Floorboards creaked under his weight. His ribs hurt and he still had a throbbing headache after the dose of laudanum wore off. But for now he ignored his aches and pains to concentrate on what lay ahead of him, listening for voices, the movement of feet on the stairs or in the lobby below.

Maybe the kid heard wrong, he thought. Or maybe it was like he told the boy, only drunk talk, bravado. If Younger had wanted to finish what he started he could have come to the hospital when Slocum was unconscious and done him in.

They came to the head of the stairs without incident and he motioned for her to wait. One slow step at a time, he began to descend to the quiet lobby. When he saw no one seated in any of the chairs arranged near a front window he waved to Myra. She came down behind him on her tiptoes.

Slocum glanced through the windows at the street out front and saw no one, an empty road cloaked in darkness. He judged it was well past four in the morning by now. Perhaps the kid's warning put him on edge for nothing. He dreaded a long walk to the livery to wake up Buck, the negro groomsman, to get a horse harnessed to a buggy, yet he knew he was too weak and sore to walk with Myra all the way to her small cottage on River Street. Thus he had no choice but to make the trip to Cobbs' Livery in the dark, leaving Myra alone in the hotel lobby until he could return.

He turned to her. "Stay here. Sit in one of these stuffed chairs and wait for me. I'll be a half hour or so. Don't leave for any reason."

"I can walk, John," she whispered, looking out every window while she said it.

He grinned down at her. "Not when you've kept company with me for an evening, Miss Reed. I always treat a lady like a lady, so sit down and wait till I get back."

She leaned forward and kissed him when she saw there was no clerk behind the desk, then she began fuss-ing with her hair as she examined her reflection in one window. "I look a mess," she said.

He wagged his head. "You're as beautiful as ever. Now sit, and stay put. I'll be back as quickly as I can."

He crossed to the twin glass doors and let himself out onto a long front porch lined with benches. Glancing up and down the street, he stepped gently, painfully, down a set of steps to the road, heading for Cobbs' Livery, his gun dangling beside his leg while he walked as fast as his injuries would allow.

He returned to the hotel at five-thirty, the pale glow of false dawn brightening eastern skies, his entire body wracked by shooting pains after the walk and climbing into the buggy seat. Even the buggy's springs were not enough to keep chugholed roads from hurting his ribs and his head, but a promise was a promise and somehow, he would manage to drive Myra home and get the carriage back.

At this hour he saw no one on the streets, a lone bakery wagon beginning early deliveries and a milk wagon crossing the bridge over the Colorado. But when he drew rein on a bay buggy horse at the Driskell's front steps, he found himself alone on the street.

Climbing down was every bit as painful as attaining the seat of the buggy had been earlier, and when faced with the steps he took a deep breath, wishing he'd remembered to bring the laudanum along. Passing the Steamboat, he noted all lamps had been extinguished and the place was closed.

"It was just tough talk over too much whiskey the boy heard before he came," Slocum told himself, using a handrail to help him climb to the porch. The death threat had come to nothing, and a long walk to the livery besides a rough buggy ride had been for nothing.

He entered the lobby quietly and froze when he saw nothing but empty chairs. Myra was nowhere in sight.

Glancing over to the Driskell's counter, he glimpsed the old man sitting at a desk with his back to the doors making notations in a ledger.

Slocum crossed the lobby quickly, sensing that something was wrong. "Excuse me, sir," he said. "A young woman was waiting here for me about an hour ago. I went to rent a carriage for her and now she's gone."

The clerk glanced over his shoulder without getting up. "I seen this tall feller in a flat brim hat an' coat walkin' a blonde-haired woman down the steps when I came out. She looked like the same lady who inquired about you right after they took you to the hospital."

"This tall fellow . . . what did he look like?"

"Didn't see much of him. Surely you can tell by these here thick glasses my eyes ain't all that good anyway. I seen he was real tall, an' he was wearin' dark clothes. One of them flat brim stetsons on his head. Coulda been he had red hair. That's about all, Mr. Slocum. Was he somebody you was expectin'?"

It was pointless to explain it fully. "It's the girl I was worried about. I was supposed to escort her home."

The old man chuckled. "Some women's that way. Another gent comes along an' before you know it, they've up an' left you. My first wife run off with a travelin' drummer. I figure I'm better off."

Slocum turned to the front windows. By the description he'd been given, he was sure Lyle Sloan was with Myra now and he had to consider the possibility that Sloan would harm her. Under ordinary circumstances he wouldn't have made it his affair. These weren't ordinary circumstances.

10

The little clapboard shack where Myra lived with her
aunt had one lamplit window at the rear of the house.
Slocum drew the rented buggy to a halt in front of the
place and eased himself down to the ground, feeling
light-headed, burdened by pain, his legs like rubber. He
leaned against the buggy's kickboard for a moment to
collect himself, then he opened a sagging gate in a picket
fence around the shack and walked to the front door.

After knocking several times, rapping his knuckles
against a door peeling whitewash, he heard a feeble
woman's voice.

"Who is it? Who's there?"

"My name's John Slocum, ma'am. I wanted to make
sure you and Myra were all right."

"I never heard of you," the voice said. "What are you
doin' bangin' on my door at six o'clock in the mornin'?"

"Jut making sure everything's okay, ma'am."

A silence.

"Ma'am? Is everything all right?" he asked again,
pulling back his coat tail so he could reach for his gun
if he needed it in a hurry.

"I ain't openin' my door for no stranger in the dark," she said, before she was stricken by a fit of wet coughing lasting a half a minute.

"Would you mind if I spoke to Myra? She doesn't have to open the door . . . all I need to know is that she's okay."

"Why wouldn't she be okay, mister? She's sound asleep in her room. She works late hours. Besides that, I don't see how it's any business of yours."

"I'm only a friend, ma'am, and I'd greatly appreciate it if you'd just look in on her, to see if she's there and feeling all right."

"Why wouldn't she be all right?" the old woman asked, then she started coughing again.

Slocum waited until her coughing spasms stopped. "I hired a carriage to bring her home, but when I got back from the livery she wasn't waiting for me. I give you my word I'm only here to be certain she made it home safely. You don't have to open the door."

More coughing fits was his only answer. He waited as the sounds moved farther away from the door. Was Myra safe in bed? he wondered. Or had Sloan taken her somewhere, perhaps to demand an answer for finding her at the Driskell Hotel lobby at five in the morning.

Dawn pinked a cloudless sky to the east, casting a curious shade of color across brightening streets and houses west of Fifth, and taller buildings in the heart of the city. And still Slocum waited, growing more impatient. Had the old woman simply gone to the back of the house, ignoring his request?

He touched his aching ribs gently, tracing a fingertip over three places where his pain was the worst. Outside the fence the bay horse stamped a hoof, rattling its snaffle bit between its teeth.

Finally, as he was turning away from the door in frustration, he heard a voice. "Go away, mister. My niece's got real bad bruises all over her face, an' she said a man she was with tonight slapped her hard. You ain't no friend of hers, or no kind of gentleman neither, to slap her that way. Her cheeks is all swole up—"

"I did not strike her, ma'am. Another man must have done it and will you please tell her I'll call on her later today, just to see how she's doing?"

"Go away! You've done enough damage for one night. I'd send for the sheriff if I could, if I had a way to get word to him."

"That won't be necessary, ma'am. I'm leaving. Just please tell Myra that John Slocum inquired about her."

He turned for his rented buggy and went through the gate in a sudden fit of rage. Now he had two scores to settle, one for himself, and one for Myra. Any man who would strike a woman was a gutless coward in Slocum's book. It was clear that Red Sloan, by the description given him by the hotel clerk, had been the one who'd blackened Myra's face.

But Slocum's anger was defeated by his injuries as he made the climb to the buggy seat. He almost blacked out, seeing stars before his eyes. He needed a dose of laudanum before he went looking for Younger and Sloan. Resting briefly against the back of the buggy seat, he finally leaned forward and picked up the reins, shaking them over the bay's rump.

The buggy lurched forward, causing more pain in his ribs and aching head. He couldn't ever recall feeling so weak, so debilitated, so helpless. As the carriage rattled toward Cobbs Livery he was forced to an unhappy decision. He needed rest as well as laudanum before he went looking for revenge.

When he returned to the Driskell he was almost too weak to climb the stairs, and after he entered his room he locked the door and took a swig of laudanum before tugging off his coat and hat. Fully clothed, he lay down on the bed gently, sweat covering him, his shirt clinging to him like a second skin despite cool fall temperatures. A moment later he passed out.

He found himself in another dream, another moment from his past. He was in Bloody Kansas with Quantrill's raiders carrying a brace of pistols, heavy Walker Colt .44s, and a Henry repeating rifle of which it was said you loaded it on Sunday and fired it all week. He held the rank of Captain, a commission given him by General Sterling Price himself, Confederate Commander of the Army of the Trans-Mississippi. But what he was doing with Quantrill's guerillas in Kansas wasn't soldiering . . . it was more like organized murder and robbery, riding alongside half-crazed killers such as Bloody Bill Anderson and men of his ilk. Slocum was a changed man, too, and he knew it. The war had hardened him, and after he lost his brother he was aware of how little capacity he had for emotion. Then a courier brought Slocum an added note of sorrow. His father had been mortally wounded while serving with the Calhoun County Militia, dying weeks later, only to be followed by his mother, who died of grief, the letter from a neighbor said. Thus Slocum found himself devoid of feelings for the most part, while the guerilla war between Northern Jayhawkers and Southern Redlegs raged on around him. He killed men, and saw hundreds of men die in Bloody Kansas, feeling nothing. And as he returned to those days in his hazy dream, he sensed his dead brother's presence as if he rode beside him. Slocum was dimly aware he was dreaming this, that it was not real, yet in some ways it felt as real as his last year in the war.

It was a bullet that ended it for Captain John Slocum,

he recalled, returning to that scene in his dream. At Lawrence, Kansas, Quantrill's atrocities were at their worst and he was there, riding beside William Clarke Quantrill, Frank and Jesse James, others who went on to infamy afterward. Quantrill led Slocum and several hundred men into Lawrence, beginning a killing spree that would last for hours until more than one hundred and fifty men and boys were gunned down in the streets. Slocum was sickened by what he saw and rode off by himself, sitting his horse, unwilling to take part in a massacre. He watched as Southerners rode down on unarmed citizens firing pistols, shouting "Kill! Kill!" as Quantrill himself did when they rode into Lawrence. A boy of fourteen or fifteen tried to escape on foot behind a blacksmith's shop where Slocum sat, watching the killing frenzy overtake men he knew were not natural-born killers. A Redleg sergeant from Mississippi Slocum knew personally spurred his horse behind the fleeing boy, aiming a pistol at the back of the youth's head as the distance closed. The boy turned, stumbling when he heard Sergeant Boyd's horse. He tried to cover his face with his hands as though his palms might somehow ward off bullets.

Boyd fired at point-blank range, flame spitting from the mouth of his .44. Slocum watching in horror as the back of the boy's skull ruptured, sending blood and brains and tufts of hair into pulpy masses flying away from his head. The youth collapsed in a heap, his legs and arms trembling with death throes, and at that very moment, something inside Captain John Slocum snapped.

"Why'd you shoot the boy? You yellow son of a bitch!" he cried as Sergeant Boyd drew his lathered horse to a halt near the body.

Boyd stared at Slocum. "What the hell's gone wrong

with you, Cap'n? We's supposed to be killin' Jayhawkers."

Slocum lifted his horse's reins to ride off. "That kid
sure as hell wasn't a Jayhawker," he spat, shaking his
head in disgust as he turned his gelding. "If we've come
down to the point where shooting children is what this
war is about, then I'm done with it."

"You called me a yellow son of a bitch, Cap'n Slocum," Boyd growled. "Weren't no call for that. We was
supposed to kill a bunch of Yank sympathizers here . . .
them was our orders, an' by God I aim to follow 'em.
Now, you take back what you said, or you're liable to
regret it. I ain't no kind of son of a bitch—"

Slocum whirled around in his saddle, glaring at Boyd
as the sounds of gunfire echoed all around them. "You're
a yellow son of a bitch for gunning down an unarmed
kid. As to the part about regretting it, the only thing I'll
regret is knowing a cowardly bastard like you. When an
order don't make any sense, only a damn fool follows
it. I won't take back a goddamn word." He glanced
down at the boy, noticing a dark stain in the crotch of
his pants when his bladder emptied with death. "Take a
good look at what you just did, Boyd. You blew that
kid's brains out and he didn't even have a gun. If those
ain't the actions of a son of a bitch and a coward, then
I'm no judge of character."

"I done warned you, Slocum."

Slocum met the sergeant's steely stare with a look of
his own. "You haven't got the balls to face a man who's
armed. If you did, I'd kill you." He touched his horse's
ribs with his boot heels and started to ride away.

He never knew from whence the bullet came, although he had every reason to believe it was Sergeant
Clayton Boyd from Mississippi who shot him. Something slammed into his back with all the force of a

mule's kick, lifting him out of his saddle. He tumbled to the ground, stunned, unable to move or raise his head. Lying on his belly, pains shooting down his spine, he felt his brother's nearness even though it was not possible . . . Robert was in a grave at Gettysburg. Slocum had dug the grave himself.

He thought he saw Robert's face, appearing as a swirl of thin smoke, an image looking down at him from above. He knew it could not be Robert and yet Robert was there, somehow.

"I can't move," he heard himself say, a voice that was not his own. "My arms and my legs won't work . . ."

Slocum was losing consciousness. He heard the sounds of a horse's hooves nearby and tried to turn his head to see who it was. Blinking, fighting the pull of unwanted sleep, he saw a fuzzy shape atop a horse, a soldier in gray with red leg bands.

His mind became a jumble of disjointed thoughts. Why was one of his own soldiers sitting there watching him? Why didn't someone come to help him? Who was this Redleg who sat motionless in his saddle while a fellow Confederate lay on the ground in need of assistance?

The figure blurred and everything went black.

In Slocum's dream he remembered every detail of the Lawrence outrage, and of the year he spent afterward as an invalid, recovering slowly, hovering near death for weeks. The dream was as real as the nightmare he experienced in Bloody Kansas back then, and now, as he revisited it in his sleep he recalled the horror of it, the boy's head exploding, the terrible agony of a bullet that struck him down and almost killed him.

Slocum awakened in a cold sweat, staring up at the ceiling of his hotel room. He turned to a window, finding it dusky and only then did he realize he'd been unconscious all day, since his return from Myra's house.

He lifted his head from the feather pillow and slowly worked his way to a sitting position on the edge of the bed with his feet touching the floor. "Damn," he whispered, remembering his dream too vividly.

A dull throbbing awakened in his ribcage, although for the moment his head was clear and free of pain. He reached for the bottle of laudanum and took a tiny sip, what he hoped would be just enough to lessen his hurting.

His room was darkening and he got up carefully to light the lantern, testing his legs while he was about the task. As soon as the wick caught he lowered the globe and took stock of his condition, finding he was still drenched with sweat. The lamp cast moving shadows on the walls as he walked to a washstand to look at his reflection, pouring water in a tin pan, dashing some of it over his face.

"You look like hell," he told himself, eyeing a lump near his temple, a scab on his chin where Younger had kicked him. A much larger lump parted his coal-black hair on the top of his head, but all in all, were it not for his sore ribs, he was in reasonable shape for a man who'd just been beaten half to death only a few days earlier. "I'll live, I reckon. I've had it a hell of a lot worse."

Turning from the mirror, he went over to one window and looked down on Fifth Street, glancing in the direction of the river. From here, he thought he could see the distant lights coming from the Steamboat Saloon. "Tonight's the night, Clay Younger," he said quietly, to himself. "And there's a dose of medicine headed for Mr. Lyle Sloan as well. You boys better be ready . . . you ain't gonna like what's comin' your way."

11

It was ten o'clock as he stood at a street corner watching the Steamboat Saloon, after stopping by the Cattleman's Club to ask about Myra. He was told a barefoot boy had come earlier to say Miss Reed wasn't feeling well, and the bartender relayed this information to Slocum with a note of concern in his voice. "She ain't hardly ever sick," the barman had said. Slocum didn't say anything about what had happened to her.

Now, as he watched the Steamboat and heard its tin kling piano and an off-key banjo being played inside, he readied for a meeting with Clay Younger and Lyle Sloan. Slocum wore a clean shirt and pants, with a crude bandage of sorts made from strips of old bed sheet binding his ribs. Underneath his coat, his gun rested in its leather holster and his small bellygun was scarcely noticeable inside his shirt.

"They'll be in there by now," he muttered, glancing up and down the street. "It's time for John Slocum to teach some school."

He crossed the road and made for the batwing doors, striding purposefully, not too quickly so as to attract attention. When he came near the doors he halted and peered cautiously through a window.

The saloon was crowded, perhaps fifty drinkers at the bar or seated around tables. Several card games were underway. Against a far wall, a badly scarred upright piano plunked out an off-key tune.

Slocum's gaze drifted to the card games, where he expected to find Sloan and Clay Younger, the man who owed him for the beating he was given in his hotel room. He saw a cowboy at one of the tables with his arm in a sling, recognizing him at once. Bob Younger sat with a handful of cards, faced so he could see the doorway. To his left, a bull-like man with a clean-shaven chin also held a hand of poker.

"That'll be Clay," Slocum whispered, feeling his heartbeat quicken with anger. Clay wore a bib front shirt covered with tobacco stains. His back was to the west wall. A battered hat was tilted back on his massive skull. Shoulder-length hair hid his shirt collar.

Slocum searched the rest of the room, looking for anyone who fit the description of Lyle Sloan. He saw no one who might have been the gunman, according to the description he had, sizing up the odds against him.

"Maybe I'm getting a break tonight. Sloan don't appear to be here yet."

Slocum opened his coat and loosened the Colt in its cross-pull berth, then he made for the doors and shouldered his way into the Steamboat. No one seemed to notice his entrance, for the moment.

Walking between tables, he made his way to a table next to the one occupied by the Younger brothers and four other card players. Suddenly, Bob looked up at him.

"Clay," Bob cried, "it's that—" Bob fell silent as Slocum drew his gun.

Slocum aimed for Clay Younger's forehead, easing

over to the wall so no one could get behind him. "Put both hands on the table," he said, moving the muzzle of his .44 back and forth between Bob and Clay. "The first son of a bitch who reaches for a gun is guaranteed to be dead. I can kill both of you before you can touch iron."

Clay's face mirrored surprise when he looked up at Slocum. His hands remained frozen around his playing cards and in the same instant, the entire saloon fell silent, the piano player being the last to notice what was going on before he ended his out-of-tune song. All eyes were on Slocum now.

Slocum's jaw jutted. "Get up, Clay," he snarled, aiming for Clay's head. "After I take the gun off you and your slow-witted brother, you and me are going outside."

Clay's eyes glittered with hatred. "You can't kill every man in this saloon, mister. You're gonna die right where you're standin'."

"Maybe," Slocum replied evenly, "but you can count on two things. Before I go down I'll kill you and your brother. You get to be first, big boy. When this forty-four puts a chunk of lead plumb through your skullbone it won't matter to you what happens next. You'll be dead. I'll drill a big tunnel all the way through your thick skull. Wherever you're headed after that, Bob is goin' with you, 'cause I can kill him too before anybody can get off a shot at me. Think about it. Are you ready to die? Any sumbitch in this place reaches for a gun, I'm gonna kill you. Understand?"

Clay's gaze flickered around nearby tables, then back to Slocum. "Don't nobody shoot," Clay said. "This crazy bastard may be just dumb enough to try it."

"Now you're showin' good sense," Slocum said, keeping one eye on Bob. "Both of you take your guns out with two fingers and put 'em on the tabletop. Anybody here does anything wrong and I put the first bullet through your brain, Clay. Anybody sneezes in this room or scratches his ass, the same thing's gonna happen."

"You gotta be outta your goddamn mind," Clay said, "comin' into a place like this by yourself, callin' me an' my brother out with a gun. You gotta be plumb crazy."

"Maybe I am," Slocum replied, feeling the danger he'd put himself in, "or maybe I'm just mad about that ass kickin' you gave me the other night in my hotel room. Either way, I'm gonna take you outside for a dose of your own medicine, or I'll kill you right where you sit. It don't make a damn bit of difference to me."

Clay glared at him defiantly, making no move to follow the order Slocum gave him to put his gun on the table.

Very slowly, in the midst of total silence in the Steamboat, Slocum thumbed back the hammer on his .44. "It's a damn shame your mouth don't reach your ass, Clay," he said, pulling a humorless grin, "so you could kiss your ass goodbye."

"Jesus, Clay," Bob croaked. "Let's take our guns out afore this crazy bastard shoots us." He took his free hand and showed it palm open to Slocum, then he reached for the butt of a .44-.40 holstered to his hip and placed it gently beside his hand of five card stud.

Slocum nodded. "Leastways there's one of you who wants to see another sunrise." His stare remained fixed on Clay. "Take your gun out, big boy, or this is *adios*."

A few quiet whispers sounded from the back of the saloon. Clay looked into Slocum's eyes, searching for an answer, or so it seemed, wondering if Slocum would actually kill him.

"You gotta be plumb fuckin' crazy," Clay said again, but as he spoke he dropped his cards and moved his right hand slowly in the direction of his pistol.

"Be real careful," Slocum warned, holding his muzzle steady aimed at Clay's forehead. "Anything happens too sudden, this gun goes off."

With his thumb and forefinger, Clay pulled out a Mason Colt .44 and put it in front of him, never once taking his eyes off Slocum's face.

"We're doin' just fine, so far," Slocum said. "Now get up, and walk in front of me to those swinging doors. This gun is gonna be right against your backbone, Clay. If either you or your brother try anything, the first bullet's gonna bust your spine." He took two steps closer to the table and gathered up both pistols with his empty hand, keeping his gun on Clay. "I won't say it again. Get up, or die in the chair." He understood this was the moment of greatest risk, when men began to move. If Clay had something up his sleeve besides an Ace, this was when he was most likely to play it. Bob's injured shoulder would keep him from acting without a weapon unless an opportunity presented itself.

Someone coughed in a corner of the place before Bob said quietly, "Come on, Clay, get up. There's gonna be another time to settle this if we do like he says."

"What'll keep him from shootin' us in the back once we get outside?" Clay wondered aloud, but as he said it he pushed back his chair.

Bob stood up, inching away from Slocum's gun muzzle. "I don't see we got no choice, Clay. You shoulda killed this son of a bitch the night you went up to his room."

Slocum kept his eyes on Clay. "Your brother's smarter than you are, Clay. And he's right . . . you should have killed me when you had the chance."

Muscles worked furiously in Clay's clamped jaw as he got to his feet. He towered above Slocum by several inches and outweighed him by at least fifty pounds.

"Head for the doors," Slocum said, backing away just enough to give the Youngers room to walk in front of him.

Bob moved first, looking over his shoulder as he took a few hesitant steps away from the table, looking at Clay. "C'mon out, Clay. This ain't no time to get mule-headed."

Clay glanced at the doors, then he shuffled heavily away from the table, dragging his boot heels over a badly stained floor.

Slocum stepped up behind Clay and placed the barrel of his gun in the small of Clay's back, prodding him with it. "Keep on movin' real slow, so I don't get nervous," he said. "This Colt has a hair trigger."

Both Youngers walked to the batwings. Bob went out ahead of Clay. Slocum followed them out on the boardwalk, stepping to one side to be out of the line of fire from the saloon if either man had a friend willing to risk a shot.

"Hold it right here, boys," Slocum said. "Bob, you take off. This is between me an' Clay. I already gave you a lesson in manners when you aimed your gun at me."

Bob glanced at his brother, then he walked away at a brisk pace, looking back until he went out of sight around one dark corner of the saloon.

Standing behind Clay, Slocum knew what he was about to do would pain his ribs some. But with seething anger prodding him on, he was willing to pay the price. He tossed both of the Youngers' pistols in the dirt below the boardwalk and as he did, he raised his gun in his right hand, bringing it crashing down across Clay's head.

"Shit!" Clay cried, stumbling forward, reaching for the spot where Slocum struck him.

Pain jolted through Slocum's ribcage as he swung again, a harder blow full of pent-up rage. The Colt's barrel made a soft, mushy sound this time when it landed on one side of Clay's skull with full force.

Clay staggered down two wooden steps to the street before his knees buckled. "Shit!" he groaned again, softer this time, sinking slowly to his knees.

Slocum looked behind him, seeing faces pressed to every windowpane of the saloon and some were peering over the tops of the batwings. He went down the steps quickly and came up to Clay, planting both feet as he prepared a powerful kick aimed for Clay's chin.

His boot toe cracked into Clay's slackened jaw—a tooth chip flew from his mouth, glimmering in lantern light from the windows. Clay spun around, arms wind-milling as he toppled over on his back with a grunt.

Slocum stepped out of a square of light from a win-dow and drove his boot heel into Clay's ribs, keeping one eye on the Steamboat's doors. He kicked Clay's ribs again, stomping downward with all his weight.

"Damn," Clay moaned, moving his hands to his belly, blood trickling from his lips.

Slocum aimed one final kick at Clay's nose, and when it landed he heard the snap of gristle and bone, moving back out of Clay's reach. Slocum's ribs burned with a fire of their own and it was all he could do to stand straight after swinging his gun so fiercely.

He looked up and down the street, then at the saloon to see if anyone was coming to Clay's rescue. When he saw no one with such an inclination headed his way, he bent down despite the raw pain in his chest and spoke to Clay. "Don't ever cross my trail again," he hissed. "If I ever see you again, if you ever so much as walk in front of me, I swear by all that's holy I'll kill you. And tell your friend Sloan that if he isn't out of town by sundown tomorrow, I'm gonna give him the same lesson for hitting the girl. He'll know what I'm talking about. Tell Sloan he's a dead man if I find him in Austin tomorrow."

Blood spewed from Clay's broken nose, but even badly hurt, he was still defiant. "I'll get you for this—"

Before the last words left Clay's mouth, Slocum drove his boot toe into Clay's throat. Clay began to choke, clasping his neck with both hands, rolling back and forth in the dirt while he gasped for breath.

"Don't threaten me, Younger, or I'll worry about it and I hate like hell to be worried. It'll be easier on me if I just kill you now, so I can get some sleep." As Slocum spoke to Clay he sensed movement in the darkness nearby. Whirling around, he was just in time to see Bob Younger running around a corner of the Steamboat with a shotgun against his shoulder.

Slocum fired instinctively, the thunder of his .44 piercing the night, echoing off storefronts. Bob became frozen in mid stride, then he began a slow dance, like he could hear the notes of a fiddler's tune. He hopped and jumped, turning this way and that, dropping the shotgun to the ground as a scream came from his throat.

Slocum's bullet had entered Bob just below his breastbone, exiting between two ribs very close to his spine. In the morning an undertaker would report to Sheriff Myers that Bob Younger probably died instantly, yet there were some who saw him do an awkward death waltz for several seconds before he went down.

Slocum walked away headed for his hotel, his gun dangling at his side. One of the Younger brothers lay dead in the street, while the other suffered a crushed larynx and was unable to speak the following day when Lyle "Red" Sloan found him to ask what had happened.

12

Lyle Sloan watched Sally undress, leaning back in a wicker-backed chair at Anna's Place with a bottle of whiskey in his fist. His black hat and coat hung on a coat tree in one corner of the upstairs room. His gaunt face bore the scar of an encounter with a knife in Hell's Half Acre, a disagreement with a Mexican *vaquero* over a palmed Ace. The Mexican was buried in a Tarrant County cemetery now. A gunbelt holding a Colt Peacemaker dangled around a bed post, a pistol with ivory grips bearing nine notches, one for each man his weapon had killed. He watched the girl, sipping whiskey now and then, fascinated by her auburn hair and milk-white skin. Sloan paid extra for this particular girl tonight, a new girl, new to the crib matron's profession. Anna often showed him favors like this because he paid more money for what he wanted.

When her bodice fell to the floor, pooling around her ankles, he beheld her ripe young breasts with a stare, as though transfixed by what he saw. "You've got real pretty tits, Sally," he said. His distinctive rasping voice made her shiver—his deep, gravelly tone had the same effect on most men and his pale gray eyes sometimes made folks nervous, especially men who found themselves in a quarrel with him. He liked his menacing appearance and traded on it at times, causing men to back down when he gave them one of his cold, hard stares.

Sally was clearly embarrassed. "Could we please turn down the lamp, mister? I ain't got used to bein' naked in front of a stranger yet."

"Hell no we can't, bitch. I paid good money an' I expect to get my money's worth. You'll stand there till I tell you to lie down. The lamp stays lit. Don't give me no argument. I wouldn't want to hurt you."

The beginnings of tears glistened in Sally's eyes. "You act real mean, mister. Miss Anna told me you were one of her best customers an' I was supposed to do exactly what you said to do, only I surely never expected to be treated bad."

"I aim to treat you the way a woman's supposed to be treated in a goddamn whorehouse. You're nothin' but a rotten cunt, to sell yourself like this. So don't give me any trouble. You're a whore, you stupid bitch. Turn around, so I can see your ass."

"Please don't get mad at me, mister," she whimpered, crying openly now.

Her obvious fear of him stiffened his swelling erection until it pulsed against the leg of his pants. He liked it when a bitch behaved like this, showing she was scared. "I'm gonna get a hell of a lot madder if you don't turn around," he growled, taking another swallow of whiskey from the neck of the bottle.

Sally turned, facing the wall, trying to stifle her sobs and control the trembling in her knees. "I'll try real hard to please you, mister," she promised in a small voice.

He admired the rounding of her buttocks, the gentler curve of her thighs, the way her long hair cascaded down her back to her slim waist. "What the hell are you shakin' for, bitch? he snapped. "Hold still so I can see what I'm payin' for."

"I'm tryin' extra hard," Sally stammered, "only you talk so mean. You've got me awful scared."

He put the bottle down and pulled off his boots, then began to unbutton his shirt. When he stood up to removed his pants the girl let out a shuddering breath, looking at his swollen cock.

"I ain't all that experienced, mister," she said, cowering against the wall near the bed. "Right at first, you'll have to put it in me real easy-like."

He dropped his trousers to the floor. "I'll put it in any goddamn way I see fit," he said, eyes glued to the swirl of dark auburn hair surrounding her cunt. "Lie down, an' shut up. I'm the one who's payin'."

Sally crept over to the mattress and lay down, spreading her thighs apart, watching him with fear in her eyes. Sloan picked up his bottle and strolled over to the bed before putting the jug to his lips, taking a long, bubbling swallow, staring at her nakedness. "You're a pretty bitch," he said, after rubbing his forearm across his mouth.

He rested the bottle on a nightstand and knelt between her legs, leering down at her, his stiff cock only inches away from Sally's pussy.

"I'm askin' you nice to put it in slow," she whimpered again as more tears came to her eyes.

He drew back a hand and slapped her hard across her cheek, instantly bringing redness to her face.

"Ow!" she cried, reaching for her face. "Please, please don't hit me no more—"

Sloan struck her other cheek with a vicious backhand blow, rocking Sally's head on the pillow. "Shut the fuck up, you no-good cunt. I'll do whatever I want." His gaze fell to her pink nipples as they turned hard. "I knew you was the type, bitch, the kind who likes a little pain along with your pleasure. See how your tits twisted up?"

He fell on top of her suddenly, ramming the head of his cock into her pussy with unnecessary force. She winced, and grabbed a fistful of bed sheet in each hand, closing her eyes tightly.

"That hurts," she groaned. "Please don't do it so hard—"

He shoved more prick inside her while pinning her arms to the bed. "How'd you like that, bitch?" he asked, pushing his shaft deeper with a sudden thrust. "Tell me how much it hurts, an' how much you like it that way."

"But I don't like—"

He cuffed her again with the heel of his hand, driving her head to one side.

"Tell me, bitch. Tell me you love it!"

"I . . . I love it, mister."

He ground his pelvis, hunching, sending more cock into her pussy savagely. Sally bit her lip to stifle a scream and kept her eyes closed. A tiny trickle of blood ran down one side of her face from her mouth.

Pumping his prick in and out, he shoved it in all the way to the hilt and felt her stiffen underneath him, although this time she did not protest or cry out for him to stop. "It feels good, don't it?" he asked.

Her lips were trembling when she said, "It feels real good, mister."

He was grunting now with each powerful thrust, banging the base of his cock against the lips of her cunt. "You're too damn dry, you lousy whore!" he complained. "How come you ain't got wet yet?"

"I'm . . . tryin' real . . . hard," she gasped between pounding thrusts, tears mingling with blood on her pillowcase as her lips continued to bleed while she cried silently.

He stopped hunching, sure of what the girl needed. "This'll help," he said, seizing her breasts in both hands, squeezing them roughly, kneading them like bread dough, then pressing down with all his weight to crush them against her chest with her nipples between his thumb and forefinger, pinching them hard.

"Oh God that hurts!" Sally exclaimed, arching her back off the mattress in spite of the crush of his long body lying on top of her.

"You know you like it," he said, chuckling, enjoying himself the way he always did with whores. "This is what you really want, you rotten bitch."

"But why?" she whimpered, sniffling back tears. "Why do you want to hurt me like this?"

"Because it's what you deserve, cunt, for offerin' to sell yourself to a man for money. You're a goddamn whore, an' you deserve to be hurt."

"That . . . don't make any sense, mister. How come you paid for me . . . when all you want to do is hurt me an' call me a whore like you been doin'?"

Sloan resumed probing her depths with his prick. "A whore oughta be put in her proper place, you stupid bitch, so you'll know what you are."

Sally winced every time his cock was buried inside her. "I only done it 'cause . . . I need money."

He slammed his cock hard against her pussy. "You turned off from honest work to make money lyin' on your back. Now earn your goddamn money an' start hunchin', or I'll hit you real hard the next time."

She tried to raise and lower her groin the way he wanted her to, finding she was pinned to the rocking mattress underneath his bulk. "I'm . . . doin' . . . the . . . best I can, mister."

Sloan increased the tempo of his thrusts when he felt his balls begin to rise—it helped to hear her crying, and to see the blood on her face. "Faster," he whispered harshly in her ear. "I want you to move faster, bitch."

Sally did her best to match his rhythm, gripping the bed sheets for all she was worth, seeking a purchase. Very gradually, wet sucking sounds came from her pussy.

"That's better," Sloan grunted.

Bed springs squeaked as he neared his climax, and now sweat poured off his face and upper body. His testicles slapped the crack of her ass, a tiny tapping sound. Warmth spread through him, his groin and thighs, his belly.

"Now, bitch, now!" he shouted, hammering his cock into her with all his strength.

A moment later his balls exploded, shooting jism into her in regular bursts, releasing intense pleasure as his scrotum emptied into her cunt.

Sloan came up suddenly on an elbow, and he slapped Sally as hard as he could across her painted lips, twisting her neck and head to one side. "There, you rotten whore!" he cried, still pumping his juices into her. "Enjoy a little pain along with your fun!"

Sally screamed, although he quickly cupped his hand over her mouth to silence her, forcing her head into the pillow as he began to suffocate her.

Her eyes bugged wide. Muffled cries came from her throat, escaping between his fingers.

"Shut up, bitch," he warned, "or I'll hit you again an' I swear it'll be a lot harder the next time."

His strokes grew shorter as the last of his jism shot into her pussy. His breathing was fast, shallow, and his temples pounded with excitement.

As soon as Sally stopped struggling he took his hand

off her mouth. He stared into her eyes. "That's a good girl," he said, his voice grating. "Be quiet now, an' let my come run down between your legs."

The girl fought to fill her lungs with air yet she remained frozen on the bed as though trapped in a block of ice, watching him with terror on her face and in her eyes.

"You see?" he asked, grinning crookedly, rising up on both elbows. "It's better with a little dose of hurtin'. All women like it."

She didn't answer him, and his grin faded. "Ain't that the truth, bitch? You liked it better 'cause I hurt you."

"Yeah . . . yes . . . anything you say, mister," Sally whispered, lying rigid, expecting another blow.

His cock softened and he pulled it out, rising back on his haunches to stare at her cunt in the lamplight. "You never did get wet, you sorry bitch," he said. "I paid way too much for dry pussy."

"I . . . tried very hard," she stammered. "I swear I done the best I could."

He got off the bed and looked down at her with disgust. "It damn sure wasn't good enough to suit me," he said, heading over to the chair to put on his pants and shirt.

Sally closed her thighs, running her tongue over a cut in her mouth. "I'm awful sorry, mister. Please don't tell Miss Anna that I wasn't no good."

He said nothing as he dressed, enjoying the begging he heard in her voice and he came close to getting another erection when he heard it. Sloan pulled on his boots, then he strapped on his gun and holster. Sally lay perfectly still, watching him as if she fully expected another slap before he left the room.

He sauntered over to the nightstand and placed an extra silver dollar beside the lamp. "I reckon it was okay for a damn whore's cunt," he said. "I'll tell Anna you wasn't half bad, for a beginner."

Sloan turned on his heel and went over to the coat tree for his coat and hat. He did not look back when he left the room.

At the bottom of the stairs, where other patrons sat talking with several of Anna's girls over wine and whiskey while seated in upholstered loveseats and chairs, he walked over to a voluptuous blonde woman in a low-cut black evening gown.

The woman spoke first. "Satisfied, Lyle?"

He nodded once, examining faces in the room. "She was one of the best, Anna. You get any more like her, you send word to me over at the Steamboat."

"I knew you'd like her. She just got to town. She said she came from some little place over in East Texas, a farm girl who wanted to make some money and see city lights. It took some tall talking to get her to agree to become . . . a woman of the night. I sent for you the moment she said 'yes' to my proposition."

Sloan tipped his hat and placed two dollars on a table next to Anna. "I'll always be real generous if you give me that kind of girl," he said, heading for the front door in a swaggering gait, pausing to look outside before stepping out on the porch, keeping his right hand close to his pistol as he went down the front steps at midnight, practicing the same caution that had kept him alive in a dangerous occupation for over a dozen years.

Once, before mounting his horse, he turned toward the center of town. While he was in the girl's room he thought he heard a distant gunshot. He supposed it could have been his imagination.

13

Slocum rested on the bed, his head propped up on two pillows with his pistol lying beside him, expecting retaliation. If Lyle Sloan came gunning for him for killing Bob Younger, he'd be ready. His Winchester stood in a corner of the darkened room, loaded, a shell in the firing chamber. His ribs ached fiercely, throbbing despite a swallow of laudanum he took when he returned to the hotel. Still, he felt better inside, where it counted. Now Clay Younger knew what sore ribs were like and his nose and throat would need time to mend.

He was certain he'd killed Bob—he saw the gunman's blue shirt pucker even in the darkness, in a spot where it would be virtually impossible for him to survive the slug. It was self defense and anyone who saw it outside the Steamboat would know the truth, that Bob had come for him with a shotgun. There would be an investigation by Sheriff Myers, no doubt, and the outcome might depend on how fearful Myers was of Clay Younger and Sloan. Sheriff Myers couldn't be trusted . . . Slocum was sure of that.

"I'll just have to see how Myers plays his cards,"

Slocum told himself, feeling the laudanum begin to do its work, a dull, numbing sensation spreading through him. He couldn't allow the medicine to let him doze off, not with the risk of retribution so high. Or would Sloan or Clay be smart enough to avoid a one-on-one confrontation with him? Clay was out of the fight, temporarily. Sloan was a gunman with a mean reputation, but was it earned? Or was he like so many others who followed the trade, an opportunist who hand-picked his victims? There was the gunman named Tucker he'd shot down, but according to the stories they had both been drunk, missing with their first shots.

Slocum listened to sounds from the street below his window while he thought about his bad luck, stopping in Austin at the wrong time. He hadn't been looking for trouble. As the years passed he made even more of an effort to avoid it. It seemed as if Lady Luck meant to dog his trail with misfortunes until his dying day. All he'd wanted in this town was a clean room and a hot bath and a few square meals. Instead, he got tangled up with two brothers named Younger and a shootist named Sloan. What he had to show for it were bruised ribs and lumps on his head, although there had been those wonderful moments in bed with Myra.

He thought about her, and promised himself he would pay her a call before he left town, no matter what else happened. The beating she took was most likely the result of her association with him and he felt he owed her that much, to call on her on his way out of the city.

"Sloan is yellow or he wouldn't hit a woman," he said to the darkness around him. "He can't be much of a man."

Slocum had dispatched Clay Younger with relative ease and when he shot Bob, it hadn't been much of a contest. The damn fool had come running around a corner in plain sight with a shotgun, Slocum remembered.

Against his wishes, he drifted off into a light sleep when the laudanum took its full effect.

A floorboard creaked in the hallway outside his door and he awakened with a start, reaching for his .44. It was still dark outside and he had no guess as to the hour. Moving quietly so as not to alert whoever was in the hall, he swung his bare feet off the bed and inched over to a corner behind the door.

Someone knocked softly, a very light tapping. He'd been expecting an attack of some kind, some form of gunplay.

"John?" a woman's voice whispered. "It's me, Myra. Can you hear me?"

He tiptoed over to the door with the Colt in his fist and paused beside the doorjam. "Are you alone?" he asked softly as the thought crossed his mind that Sloan might have forced her to become a decoy.

"Yes. I slipped out after my aunt went to sleep. I can only stay a minute. I wanted to explain—"

Something in her voice allowed him to trust her. He turned the key and opened the door.

Myra stood in the poorly lit hallway with the same light shawl around her shoulders. She was alone. Even in the half dark he could see bruises on her face and a swollen lower lip.

"Come in," he said, lowering his gun, looking past her down the hall to make sure it was empty. "I had a little run-in with Clay Younger and his brother, so you'll have to excuse me if I seem a mite jumpy."

Myra came into the room smelling of sweet perfume, a lilac scent. Before he could close the door, she kissed him lightly on the cheek. "What happened?" she asked, sounding fearful now.

Slocum locked the door. He stared at her a moment. "Your face looks a mess. I know it was Sloan who hit you—"

"He flew into a fit of jealous rage when he found me down in the lobby. He grabbed my arm an' pulled me outside, then he hit me a bunch of times, callin' me awful names. He wanted to know who I was with at the hotel, only I wouldn't tell him. He hit me so hard I blacked out. I woke up when he had me across his horse takin' me home. He threw me to the ground an' called me a whore, then he rode off. But I figure he knows by now I was with you an' I came to warn you. He's god-awful mean, John, an' I sure wouldn't want him to hurt you." She let her shawl drop off her shoulders, moving closer to him. "It's gonna sound silly, but I think I love you, John. I couldn't have it on my conscience if he did somethin' to you. I know you'll be leavin' town soon an' I never expected anything to come of this, of us. But a woman can still love a man even if she can't keep him. You aren't the settlin' down kind an' I know it. But I still love you."

He smiled and took her in his arms with his pistol still dangling from his right hand, holding it behind her back. "Let me set you straight on a few things, pretty lady," he began. "I know how to take care of myself, so don't worry about me if Lyle Sloan shows up. Secondly, I've got strong feelings for you, too, only I'm not rightly sure what love is. There'll come a time when I'm ready to settle down in one place, and when that time arrives I may come calling. In the meantime, I won't tolerate a man hitting a woman friend of mine, don't matter who he claims to be. Before I leave town I'll have a little talk with Sloan, to get it through his head he can't hit a woman I call a friend. He won't ever strike you again. You've got my word on that."

"He's a dangerous killer, John. I heard all the stories about men he killed. He shot a man here in Austin an' I wouldn't be able to stand it if he did the same to you. Until the other night he'd been nearly a perfect gentleman around me. Then the jealousy came out in him."

"Jealous or not, I won't let him hit you. If he's still in town tomorrow, I intend to give him a little reminder, so he'll think twice before he strikes a defenseless woman again."

She rested her head against his chest. "You don't owe me a thing. I suppose I had it comin', only you were so charmin' an' all, I guess I couldn't help myself."

Slocum held her close. "What happened between you and me is private. We did what came natural at the time." He could feel her taut breasts against his chest, her hard nipples bringing a stirring to his groin even though he still felt groggy from the laudanum.

Myra drew back and looked up at him. "How come you ain't afraid of Lyle?" she asked. "Everybody else in town is scared of him, includin' the sheriff."

He considered his answer carefully before he gave it. "I've never met a man I was afraid of. Met a few I respected because they were good with a gun and did my best to avoid having any trouble with 'em. After the war I suppose I'd seen enough of death so that dying didn't frighten me, like it does some folks I've known. If another man kills me in a fight, I earned it for getting in that fight in the first place. But as to the scared part, I'm just not made that way."

She reached for his crotch, fingering his cock through his undershorts. "You're one hell of a man, John Slocum. You've got what it takes to please a woman, in more ways than one. You're a true gentleman . . ." She sighed. "And you're the best lover I've ever had, an' I was deeply touched when you came by our house to see how I was. I couldn't come to the door. My face was a bloody mess, all swollen up. I didn't want you to see me lookin' like that. I look bad enough right now, but the swellin's gone down some."

"You look beautiful," he told her, as his prick began to rise. "It don't matter about the bruises. They'll heal. You are still a very lovely woman."

Myra went slowly to her knees, opening his fly to take out his swelling erection. She looked up at him briefly, then she put the head of his cock between her lips, flicking her tongue in and out, back and forth. A moment later she pulled back. "This makes me a very naughty person, doesn't it?" she asked, stroking his shaft with one hand.

"No," he whispered, feeling heat build in his balls. "It makes you a very sensual woman."

"Move over to the bed," she said, her voice thickening with desire. "I want to show you just how sensual I can be with a man I love."

He backed over to the edge of the mattress and sat gingerly to avoid hurting his ribs. Myra held firmly to his cock, coming with him on her knees. When he was seated on the mattress she put his prick in her mouth again, deeper this time, moving her head up and down slowly, making sucking sounds. He spread his legs, resting on his palms, watching the beautiful girl give him incredible sensations with her tongue and lips.

"That feels so good," he breathed.

She did not answer. The sucking noises grew louder and her tongue worked faster and faster.

Warm saliva dripped down the length of his shaft, trickling onto his testicles while her head bobbed. Then a moaning sound came from deep in her throat.

He reached for her free hand and placed it gently below his balls, cupping her fingers around them. Myra got the idea at once and began to stroke his testicles softly, lifting them higher.

"Perfect," he whispered, tightening the muscles in his buttocks.

Myra's rhythm increased, her head moving up and down his shaft at greater speed. Her tongue encircled the head of his cock and spasms of pleasure gripped him, intensifying, building to a climax.

"I can't stand it much longer," he said, grinding his teeth when passion threatened to drive him over the edge.

She moaned again, working her head furiously, rubbing his testicles, flicking her tongue.

His balls released a fountain of jism, filling her mouth as his spine and legs went rigid, his feet rising off the floor so his knees were locked. "Oh darlin'!" he exclaimed, trembling, limbs stiffened in ecstasy.

Come ran down the shaft of his prick when Myra's mouth was overflowing and yet she still pumped his shaft with her fingers, asking for more. Jacking him harder and harder, she drew the last drops of jism from him before she slowly withdrew her mouth from his cock.

His body went slack, his passion spent. He was gasping for each breath.

"Was it good?" she asked, gazing up at him, licking her lips as a slow smile crossed her face.

"It doesn't get any better," he said, as all the tension went out of him. He felt completely drained.

Myra stood up, unbuttoning her blouse, her shawl falling to the floor. "It's my turn now," she said playfully. "Just lie down on your back like you did before."

He followed her instructions, easing himself down on the mattress. Myra wriggled out of her skirt and it was then he noticed she wasn't wearing a bodice.

She knelt beside him on the bed, completely naked, taking his limp cock in one hand, fingering it gently.

"It may take a minute," he explained.

"We've got plenty of time before my aunt wakes up. Lie still an' quit worryin'."

"Sometimes a man can't—"

She hushed him with a finger to her moist lips, then she bent over his prick and licked the head of it with the tip of her tongue. Her hot mouth worked like magic, and within seconds he felt the beginnings of another erection.

"You sure as hell know what you're doing, pretty lady," he said."

She halted the motion of her mouth. "It's because I like what I'm doin', my dear," she replied, then her tongue went back to work on his glans.

His cock came erect in pulsating jerks, but when Myra put it on her tongue, a rush of blood filled it, engorging every thick inch of it.

"That's much better," Myra whispered, climbing on top of him, inserting his cock into the damp lips of her silky mound. "Oh yes!" she sighed, grinding down on his length a little bit at a time.

He gazed up at her, certain that among all the women he'd known, Myra Reed loved her pleasure as much or more than any of them.

14

Before Myra left his room at the crack of dawn they agreed to a picnic lunch that afternoon somewhere along the banks of the Colorado. He promised to rent a buggy and pick her up at noon with the understanding that if he wasn't at her house at the appointed hour, it would be because of last night's shooting and she shouldn't worry. He told her he didn't expect problems with Sheriff Myers over it, not with so many witnesses watching the affair at the Steamboat. What he failed to tell her was a possibility that the sheriff might take another view of things, fearing what Clay Younger and Lyle Sloan might do before Slocum left town.

"You watch out for Lyle," she'd said, kissing him tenderly before she left to hurry home. "Now that I've seen that mean streak in him, I'll worry what he might do to you, knowing you an' I've been together."

He had reassured her as best he could, without telling her that if Sloan called him out over it, Slocum would be glad to oblige. Nor did he tell her about the threat he made, telling Clay that if Sloan crossed his path in the future he would make him pay dearly for striking Myra.

He was strolling down Sixth Street toward the Capitol Cafe when he saw Sheriff Myers headed his way. It was after ten in the morning and Slocum felt better, rested, experiencing less pain.

"I need a word with you, Mr. Slocum," Myers said, halting him on a boardwalk in front of a harness shop. "No need to explain why you done it, but you killed a man last night."

"It was self-defense, Sheriff. There were dozens of witnesses at the Steamboat. He came at me with a shotgun. It was him, or me."

Myers scowled. "That ain't the way some folks are tellin' it. A couple of gents are swearin' Bob was unarmed."

"They're liars. The shotgun was lying right there beside him when I started back to the hotel."

"Wasn't no gun there when the undertaker's wagon came, an' he wasn't carryin' a pistol either."

"I disarmed both of the Younger brothers. I walked them out of the place and told Bob to disappear if he didn't want any more trouble with me. Then I swatted Clay over the head a few times, just like he done to me."

Myers appeared nervous. "Until I get to the bottom of it, I'm orderin' you not to leave town. I may have to take you over to the District Attorney so charges can be filed, unless I can find somebody who'll back up your story."

Slocum's temper flared. "You said you wanted rid of them in this town, and now you tell me I may face murder charges for shootin' one of them who tried to kill me with a shotgun. You're talking out both sides of your mouth."

The sheriff looked around to see who was listening. "If I tell you I ain't the least bit sorry you killed that bastard, it won't be official, you understand. But there's some here who act real scared of what Clay Younger an' Red Sloan will do if I don't file murder charges against you. It's like this . . . you're a total stranger in this town, an' you'll be leavin' soon. Clay an' Red won't go no place unless somebody makes 'em, an' I can't get no help to get that done. I wouldn't stand a chance against those boys. I'd be as dead as Bob, if'n I tried. So I'm in a fix, so to speak. A few concerned citizens an' a member or two of the city council want you arrested an' charged with killin' an unarmed man."

"The charges would be false, trumped-up. Every man who was in the Steamboat saw what happened." Slocum tried to control his anger. Austin's spineless sheriff was showing off his true colors.

Myers looked down at his boots. "Findin' one who'll tell the truth is gonna be the problem. Everybody's scared of Clay an' Sloan . . . what they'll do if anybody talks."

Slocum put his hands on his hips. "You're supposed to be the law in this town. Are you gonna let these two-bit owlhoots run things?"

The sheriff's face paled. He continued to avoid Slocum's piercing stare. "I never counted on somethin' like this, an' I believed folks would stand behind me if a bunch of bad actors came to town. I was promised a full-time deputy an' support from this community. Instead, nearly every damn one of 'em left me high an' dry when this trouble started. Nobody wanted this job after the other sheriff got his head blowed off. I figured I'd have some backin' from good citizens if I pinned on this star, but you can see I ain't got any."

Hearing Myers explain his dilemma, Slocum softened a bit and cooled down. "Look, Sheriff, there has to be somebody who was at the Steamboat last night who'll tell the truth about what happened. They can't all be too frightened to talk."

Myers wagged his head. "You don't know these folks like I do. But I'll keep askin'. To tell the honest truth, as little as I know about you, there's no way I'd believe you'd shoot an unarmed man. Trouble is, what I think won't count for much. I can promise you this . . . I'll do the best I can to find somebody who'll say he seen Bob Younger with a gun. Until then, I'm gonna have to ask you to stay."

Slocum eyed the front of the cafe. "I'll give you until tomorrow, Sheriff. If you don't find a witness who'll tell the truth, I'll do some looking on my own."

He stepped around Sheriff Myers to get some coffee and then walked to the livery to rent a buggy. Despite this sudden turn of events he was still looking forward to the picnic with Myra.

A two-rut lane wound its way beside the river, shaded by towering oaks shedding fall leaves when gusts of wind came from the north. Myra sat beside him on the buggy seat with a picnic basket, her leg touching his. Overhead a sky full of puffy white clouds painted a beautiful background for the forest's colors. To their right, the Colorado moved sluggishly toward the Gulf of Mexico. Cottonwoods and pecan trees and slender-leafed elm stood along the banks, leaves turned to brilliant reds, bright yellows and softer browns, swirling on irregular currents of cool air like tiny dervishes until they touched the ground. Tall cliffs of pale limestone rose more than a hundred feet high on the west side of the river, some cloaked in deep green vines not yet changing colors with the coming of winter.

"There's a pretty spring not far up this road," Myra said, smiling up at him. "It's a nice place for a picnic.

Quiet. I used to go there a lot when I was younger. It's a place where I could think an' be all to myself."

When he listened to her voice now it had a musical quality, almost girlish. He wondered why she never married. "How is it that a beautiful woman like you never took a husband?" he asked, hoping he wasn't opening old wounds.

The smile left her face. She stared blankly at the lane for a time. "I had a beau once. Seems like a long time ago. We'd talked about gettin' married some day. Then my aunt got sick. My pa died when I was eleven, so we were always alone, just the two of us. Nell did sewing an' took in laundry. Billy wanted me to marry him an' move to Fort Worth, where he got this job with a cattle buyer. I told him I couldn't leave my aunt, her bein' so sick an' all. The doctor told her she was gonna die, that it was only a matter of time. Wasn't nothin' he could do. Billy begged me to go with him an' be his wife. I just couldn't. He left for Fort Worth three years ago. I haven't heard from him since. So long as my aunt's alive, I have to take care of her. She's real weak now . . . can't hardly dress herself, even. Doc Hardin said it was only gonna be a few more months before . . ." Her voice trailed off and a tear sparkled in the corner of her eye.

"Sounds like you and your aunt have had more than your fair share of misfortune," he said quietly, guiding the buggy horse around a tree in the road. "If she's suffering, it may be for the best when it's over."

"She's hurtin' real bad these days. The doctor gives her morphine, when we can afford it. I don't make all that much at the Cattleman's Club. We get by."

Slocum felt genuine sympathy for her, hearing her story. A time or two he glanced over at her, noting the bruises on her face from the beating Sloan gave her. He found himself filled with more resolve than ever to teach Sloan some manners, or kill him if the gunman wouldn't have it any other way. Slocum was in a blind rage when he told Clay he meant to kill Sloan if they ever crossed paths. Today he he felt a bit differently, some of his anger melted away. He decided to prepare Myra for what could happen if charges were filed against him. "I talked to Sheriff Myers this morning. He told me all the witnesses to the gunshot I fired at Bob Younger are saying he was unarmed. I might be charged with murder, unless someone steps forward to tell the truth."

"Oh, John," she whispered, gripping his arm. "A jury could send you to prison, or even hang you."

He slapped the bay's croup with one rein to quicken its gait a little. "I'll find somebody who'll tell the truth. I can't believe every man who saw it is afraid of Clay, or this Sloan."

Myra's eyes filled with worry. "Lyle supposedly killed a man as soon as he came to town, a man named Tucker who folks said was fast with a gun an' mean-dispositioned to boot. That's what I heard, anyways, only I guess I didn't want to believe it about him, 'cause he was so nice to me . . . right at first."

"I heard the story myself," Slocum said, "only Tucker and Sloan were both too drunk to shoot straight. Sloan may have gotten lucky that night."

"I've been so worried he'll come lookin' for you, now that he knows I'm keepin' company with someone else."

He didn't respond, having already explained why he wasn't afraid of that possibility.

A bluejay screeched from a nearby limb, fluttering off as the buggy came closer. Near the base of a limestone cliff a gray squirrel chattered, arcing its tail over its back as a warning to others that an intruder was in the forest. On this seldom traveled lane they saw no one, no houses, no signs of civilization and Slocum found he liked the peace, the quiet.

"Over there," Myra said, pointing to an opening in the trees. "The spring's at the bottom of that pile of rocks. It always runs clear an' cold . . . the water tastes sweet, like it's got sugar in it."

He chuckled and swung the buggy horse off the lane at a walk as they passed between thick oak trunks. Just ahead, he could see a small pool of water in a hollow beside a pile of boulders fallen from cliffs above.

Slocum halted the buggy beside a clear, shallow spring at the headwaters of a tiny creek. Cattails and reeds grew around the edges of the pool, and even before he got down to help Myra from the buggy seat, he saw fish darting between water plants growing beneath the surface.

"Isn't it pretty here?" she asked as he took her hand to assist her.

"One of the prettiest places I've ever seen," he said, "a perfect place for a quiet picnic with a beautiful woman."

She lowered her face. "I'm not pretty now," she told him softly. "My face looks ugly, after what Lyle did."

He took her chin and raised it with his fingertips, then he bent down and kissed her. "You've never been ugly a day in your life, Miss Reed. The marks on your cheeks will go away." He gave her a grin and took the picnic basket from the floorboard.

"Over here," Myra said, pointing to a grassy spot where a few shafts of warm sunlight spilled between heavy branches. "I used to sit in that spot when I was lonely, or needin' to think about things."

Slocum reached under the seat and took out a fresh bottle of imported cognac. He laughed out loud when he remembered he'd forgotten to bring glasses. "You'll have to drink out of the jug this time," he said. "I forgot glasses."

"It won't matter," she replied, taking a folded table-cloth from her basket to spread on the ground where the sun shone the brightest. "I fixed biscuits an' sausage, an' brought along some cheese an' crackers. I made pecan pralines for dessert."

He brought the bottle over, took off his coat while being careful not to stretch his ribs, and squatted down at the edge of the cloth as Myra spread food before him.

"You shouldn't have gone to so much trouble," he told her. "All I really wanted was to spend some time with you."

She smiled and blushed. "You say the sweetest things, John Slocum, like honey just drips from your tongue. An' best of all you make me feel pretty. Here, have a sausage sandwich an' I'll cut you a piece of cheese."

He took the biscuit and bit into it, chewing as he watched her nibble daintily on a piece of cheese. Between bites he twisted the cork from their cognac and offered the bottle to her with a smile. "The sandwich is delicious," he said, watching Myra raise the bottle to her lips and the way the light played through her golden hair, making it sparkle like sapphires were hidden in her curls.

He took the cognac and drank deeply, only slightly bothered by his ribs today. As he corked the bottle he glanced up at the rim of a limestone bluff overlooking the river.

A horseman in a flat brim hat was looking down on them, and in a flash Slocum knew who he was. Trouble had followed them to this pristine spot, and today, trouble had a name.

15

"Get down behind those rocks!" Slocum snapped, keeping his voice low. "We've got company."

Myra turned her head toward the bluff. "Oh my God!" she exclaimed. "It's Lyle—"

"Get to cover," Slocum insisted while reaching for his Colt, certain that the range was too great for any accuracy. If Sloan had a rifle he would be a sitting duck. "Move!" he cried, coming quickly to his feet, heading for a massive oak trunk that would offer him protection and draw fire away from the girl.

He reached the tree with his heart pounding, peering around it with his .44 aimed up at the rim just as Myra scurried behind a pile of boulders. The gunshots Slocum expected did not come. Sloan sat on his horse, silhouetted against blue sky, an ominous shape at the edge of the cliff, frozen in place like a vulture perched on a limb.

What the hell's he waiting for? Slocum wondered. A good marksman with a rifle could have easily hit a target from his vantage point.

"I just knew this would happen," Myra sobbed, crying, her hands covering her mouth and nose.

"Just stay put and be quiet," Slocum said, watching Sloan for his next move. "He didn't shoot, so maybe he's just trying to throw a scare into us."

"Why won't he leave us alone?" she whimpered, peeking above the top of a rock.

"I reckon it's because he thinks you're his property, his woman," Slocum answered, still puzzled by the gunman's behavior.

Sloan looked down from the bluff. Slocum had no guess as to how long he'd been watching them. If Sloan meant to kill him for being with Myra, then why was he waiting? Was he so cock-sure of himself that he was enjoying this, hoping to make his prey sweat blood before he attempted to end it?

For half a minute more the gunman remained in plain sight on the rim, then he lifted his reins slowly and swung his horse away from the bluff, disappearing behind the rock ledge.

"He's gone," Myra said, her voice tight with fear. "I just know he's comin' down here, ridin' around the back of that cliff to come after me an' you." She looked across at Slocum. "I'm so sorry I brought you out here, John. It was such a nice day for a picnic . . . an' I wanted so much to be with you. I never dreamed he would be watchin' us, followin' us."

"Let him come," Slocum told her, backing away from the tree while still watching the top of the bluff. "The closer he gets the bigger his mistake is gonna be. I never thought to bring my rifle. Pack up your picnic basket. If he don't show up in a half hour or so we'll head back to town, only we'll have to go real slow and careful in case he aims to ambush us. I'm the one he wants."

"He's comin'," she promised, edging away from the boulders. "When he gets mad like he did that mornin' when he found me at the hotel, he carries on like a different person, like he's got somethin' wrong inside his head. His eyes get this funny look. It's hard to describe it so you'll understand. When he introduced himself at the Cattleman's Club, he behaved like a perfect gentleman. He brought me a box of sweets the next time, an' we went for a walk in the moonlight. I let him kiss me, an' he told me I acted like a real lady's supposed to. He said if I wanted I could go with him to San Francisco in the spring, to see all the fancy opera houses an' street cars, the Pacific Ocean, too. He told me we'd ride the train, an' it got me to dreamin' about all those things."

Slocum was scanning the forest around them, any place where a horseman might ride down from the cliffs. Dense stands of oak and pecan made it difficult to see where light and shadow played tricks on a man's eyes. "Sounds like he had you love-struck," he said without turning around.

He heard her footfalls coming up behind him. "You're the only man I've fallen in love with since Billy," she said as she touched his arm. "The thing with Lyle was never serious. He knew all the right things to say, but I always felt there was somethin' about him I shouldn't trust. Now I know I was right to believe that. He showed me just how mean he can be. Maybe I deserved it, for goin' up to your room. I only know that from the moment I met you, I felt somethin' inside."

He glanced back at her and smiled reassuringly. "Maybe it was destiny that we met." Slocum turned to the forest again. "I want you to pack your basket. I can't quite figure what Sloan is up to, but I won't give him the chance to bring you any harm. As soon as you're ready, I want you to hide behind those rocks again while I scout the road back to town. If it looks clear, we'll head back."

"Please be careful," she said, rising on her toes to kiss his cheek before she went to the basket to put their food and the tablecloth away.

When the basket was in the floorboard of the buggy he made a motion toward boulders above the spring. "Stay down and be quiet till I get back. No matter what happens, no matter what you hear or see, don't leave that spot. I'll be back in a few minutes, as soon as I take a look down this lane."

He moved silently into the forest, practicing an art he'd mastered years ago stalking wild game in Calhoun County. Placing each boot carefully to avoid dry twigs and leaves, staying where shadows from tree limbs made him harder to see, he inched down to the lane beside the river and waited, his .44 clamped in his fist while he listened, searching for anything that seemed out of place, trusting his senses. When he paused behind a tree he made himself wait, examining every bush, every rock, any spot where a bushwhacker could hide.

"Something don't feel right about this," he whispered, after a lingering look at his surroundings.

He crept forward again, dodging back and forth, remaining still for several seconds at a time before he moved again. In a dark corner of his brain a small voice told him there was danger ahead and yet no matter how closely he looked, he found nothing wrong and slowly he began to question his inner feeling that something was amiss.

Slocum covered a half a mile of roadway before relaxed and shook his head. Birds chirped from tree limbs in the forest, a sign they were aware of no other presence. Squirrels scampered from his path, watching him, paying no heed to anything else in the river bottom.

He took a deep breath, scanning the two-rut road

winding among the trees. A cottontail rabbit sat in one of the ruts nibbling grass. "Nobody's there," Slocum said. Wild animals were the first to sense a threat and their eyesight and hearing, as well as their sense of smell, was far keener than his.

He gave up and turned around, plodding back down the road toward the spring, bewildered by the false alarm his senses had given him. He'd been so sure someone was close by, that Sloan had set a trap for them and he wondered how he could have been so wrong. Keeping to the shadows, no longer concerned about the noises he made, he trudged slowly beside the Colorado puzzling over the gunman's actions. Why had he shown himself so plainly before? The only possible answer was that he hoped to scare Slocum away from Myra, or frighten her into staying wide of Slocum. It was disconcerting after a fashion, that he'd been fooled by his own survival instincts, that feeling he got when his life was in danger. "Maybe I'm really getting old," he said quietly, "afraid of my own damn shadow."

Keeping an eye on his backtrail, he made his way toward the spring. He'd gone only a few hundred yards when he heard Myra scream.

"Son of a bitch," he muttered, breaking into a run, even though haste made the pain in his ribs awaken suddenly. He ran as fast as he could, ignoring all caution, racing toward the thin wail of Myra's voice.

Her shrill scream ended abruptly, followed by the distant crack of a gunshot and the sound was like an arrow through his heart. Above all else he'd wanted to keep harm from coming to the girl and judging by the sound, Sloan must have shot her.

"I knew the bastard was yellow," Slocum wheezed, huffing and puffing to maintain his lumbering run with injuries slowing him down. "I swear I'm gonna kill that son of a bitch, no matter how far he runs."

His sides were aching by the time he reached the opening in oak trunks leading to the pool. Fifty yards ahead, sitting in mottled sunlight shining between branches, he caught a glimpse of the buggy's black canvas canopy near the jumble of boulders where he'd tied off the harness horse. But as he drew nearer, what he saw brought him up short . . . the buggy horse lay crumpled between the buggy shafts, its legs flailing, hopelessly tangled in bits of leather harness strap and driving reins.

Halting beside a tree, he required a moment to understand what he was seeing, what had happened. "He shot the horse," Slocum gasped, cocking an ear when he heard distant hoofbeats moving farther away. "Why the hell would he shoot a horse when he coulda killed her?"

All too quickly, things fell into place. He swept a glance around the clearing encircling the spring. Myra's picnic basket lay on its side, its contents scattered about in the grass.

"He's got her," Slocum said under his breath. "He took her with him and he killed the horse so I couldn't follow him. He suckered me into leaving her alone and that's exactly what the bastard wanted me to do."

Now the hoofbeats were gone. Slocum lowered his pistol to his side, panting, trying to catch his breath. He was furious with himself. "He took me in like I was a goddamn greenhorn," he mumbled. Being afoot, with sore ribs, there was no way he could follow the gunman's tracks to make any attempt at rescuing Myra.

A few moments later he walked slowly into the clearing to put the horse out of its misery with a bullet—he couldn't bear to watch it. At times like these he wondered why he felt nothing when he shot a man, and experienced so much sorrow when he was forced to kill an animal. He supposed it was because the men he killed were his enemies, even back in the war when killing other Americans who happened to live north of the Mason-Dixon line were his orders, because they were considered enemies, even though the cause they fought and died for made as little sense as the one he fought to preserve. But killing animals, especially horses, which he had a special fondness for, seemed so much more painful. He only hunted game such as deer or elk or wild turkey, when he was hungry, needing meat to survive in the wilderness. Even after all these years, he had some difficulty sorting through what was an apparent contradiction.

Slocum walked over to the bay buggy horse and aimed the barrel of his gun into the dying gelding's right ear, thus the bullet did not have to penetrate thick skull bone to do its act of kindness.

"Sorry," he whispered just before he pulled the trigger, looking away so he wouldn't see the horse's death throes any longer.

His gunshot resounded off the limestone cliff above him and at last, the gelding lay still.

Walking down the lane toward Austin, he cursed his stupidity for leaving the girl alone. Because of it, because of him, she would probably suffer another terrible beating. She might even lose her life due to his carelessness.

The closer to town he came, the madder he got, even though he knew as well as any man that anger caused men to make mistakes. When John Slocum got mad, he'd also been known to discard wisdom in favor of vengeance.

●   ●   ●

Sheriff Myers paled. "There simply ain't anythin' I can do, Mr. Slocum. I don't stand no kind of chance goin' up against a gent like Red Sloan. You say this trouble is over a woman. I figure the best thing you can do is ride on to wherever it was you was headed an' let Sloan an' the woman settle it."

Slocum's jaw jutted in an angry line. "You have to be the most gutless man I ever met who wore a badge, Myers. You've got a responsibility to the citizens of this town."

The sheriff tried to sound stern. "You can't talk to me like that. Besides, you're still under investigation for murder here. I'm offerin' you a chance to ride away from it, an' instead you tell me I've got responsibilities, that I'm gutless."

Slocum turned for the door into the sheriff's office. "I'll handle it myself," he said, biting down. "Tell me one thing. I need to know where Sloan is staying the night, a rooming house, a hotel."

Myers shrugged. "I never wanted to know, but I have heard it said he's been seen at Anna's several times. It's a whorehouse. He goes there late at night when he's needin' a woman."

Slocum jerked the door open to go outside. "He's already got a woman, a prisoner being held against her wishes. Unless I'm wrong, he'll hurt her pretty bad, if he hasn't done anything to her already." He gave Myers a cold stare. "You're one hell of a sorry excuse for a lawman," he added, stalking out, slamming the door behind him.

He stormed along the boardwalks toward the Driskell Hotel to fetch his rifle, then to the livery to saddle his horse. He was on the prod, hell-bent on finding Myra, hoping he wasn't too late to help her. One thing he was absolutely certain of—he wouldn't be leaving Austin until he found her and Lyle Sloan, and when he did, no matter how long it took, he swore to put a hole through Sloan and hang around town long enough to attend his funeral.

16

Cobbs eyed him carefully when Slocum walked into the barn at 4 o'clock balancing a Winchester in his hand. Slocum spoke to the stable owner as he headed for the saddle shed. "I owe you for a rented bay gelding. Your carriage is about two miles up the Colorado next to a spring below a limestone ledge. Lyle Sloan shot the horse. I should get a bank wire tomorrow so I can pay for the animal. Right now I'm a little short of funds."

"Why would Sloan shoot my buggy horse?" Cobbs inquired with a scowl creasing his face.

"He meant to keep me from following him when he took the girl, Myra Reed, with him. We were having a picnic. He found a way to trick me into leaving the girl alone a moment while I looked for him, figuring he'd try to bushwhack me on our way to town. I'm sorry about the horse and the inconvenience. I'll pay all reasonable charges."

"I'll send Buck out with a spare horse for the buggy, Mr. Slocum. Remember I warned you about Myra, an' Sloan, an' them Younger brothers. Everybody's talkin' about how you killed Bob in front of the Steamboat, an' they say you gave Clay one hell of a beatin', too. Clay's gonna be dangerous as soon as he heals up. You'll have both him an' Sloan to contend with. It ain't my place to say it, but you may have bitten off more'n you can chew."

The remark should have angered him, though he was already mad enough to bite a nail in half, thinking about how Sloan had fooled him. "I can chew it," was all he said, wincing when he took his saddle off a saddle rail. "I told the sheriff what happened. It was wasted breath. Maybe you know something that can help me. Any idea where Sloan stays when he ain't at the Steamboat?"

Cobbs nodded. "A roomin' house at the corner of Second Street called Lilly's, only he wouldn't be crazy enough to take her there. Clay an' Bob rented a shack by the river. Used to be the old Kelton place. Wilber Kelton got killed in the war. It's south of the bridge. Got a pole corral an' a shed out back. You'll see a big red sorrel geldin' in the pens . . . it's Clay's. Can't miss it if you ride along the river just south of the bridge. By the way, they're gonna have the funeral tomorrow for Bob Younger. It was wrote up in the newspaper."

Slocum went to the stall and bridled his stallion, feeling footsore after walking back to town, then to the livery. His stud looked fresh, rested, well-fed. He ignored the news of a funeral for Bob Younger, not finding anything about it worth mentioning to the liveryman. Slocum had been the one who put Bob Younger in a pine box, and as soon as he located Lyle Sloan, an undertaker would be digging another hole in the city cemetery.

He led the horse out and swung his saddle over its withers with a great deal of pain spiking his chest. Pulling the cinch was no easier. Slocum booted his rifle and led the stud out in late afternoon sunshine before he mounted.

Cobbs watched him step into the saddle. "You look like a man who's hell-bent on starin' the devil in the eye," he said, rolling a straw stem across his tongue. "You proved to plenty of folks in this town that you're tough, but mister, I'd think twice before I ran headlong into Red Sloan. Them Younger boys was plain mean, an' Clay's big enough to get his way bein' so strong an' bad-natured. But Sloan is another breed, a killer by profession, an' he won't make very many mistakes, accordin' to the tales from up in Hell's Half Acre at Fort Worth about him. I ain't tellin' you your business. It's your neck, but if I was you I'd think real hard about whether that woman is worth dyin' for."

Slocum swung a glance toward the river and the bridge while gathering his reins. "I appreciate your advice, Mr. Cobbs, but I don't need to think hard about whether or not I'll pay a call on Sloan. I've been staring the devil in the eye, as you call it, most of my life, and I've found out a thing or two about Satan and his disciples. They ain't real fond of facing a man who keeps on a-comin', no matter what. Sloan and Clay Younger are about to find out I'm a real hard man to kill."

He turned his horse for the Colorado, riding at an easy gait to spare his aching ribs. When he saw the river, Slocum's eyes became slits and that same blazing temper that had gotten him in difficulties the better part of his life began building into an inferno, beyond his control.

A red sunset bathed the river bottom with crimson light, casting its hues over small houses and shacks built along the river bank, mirrored on the glassy surface of the water, pink where it fell on whitewashed walls and fences. Tall canebrakes stood in clusters near the water's edge. Cattails and reeds thickened in backwater eddies and below cutbanks. Behind him, heavy freight wagons rumbled over oak planks flooring the old bridge. Slocum rode down a narrow roadway between ramshackle cabins, one of the poorest sections of town, looking for a big sorrel gelding in livestock pens behind the shacks. Chickens pecked the dirt for a few final seeds before going to roost, scattering from his stallion's path when he rode toward them, flapping their wings, clucking and squawking noisily over his intrusion. Somewhere close by, pigs grunted and squealed. Seated on a sheer drop in the river bank, a fisherman clad in overalls watched him ride past while attending to three cane fishing poles. Slocum noticed all these things without allowing any of it to distract him, searching for a red gelding and a shack where he might find out where Sloan had taken the girl.

A few hundred yards south of the bridge he spotted a big sorrel with a flaxen mane and tail, standing in a tumbledown corral chewing a mouthful of hay. He reined back on the stud, examining the little slant-roofed house in front of the pen.

Windows were dark, although it might be early for a lantern yet. Slocum pulled the hammer thong off his Colt and swung out of the saddle.

Just one horse in the corral, he thought. Sloan isn't here now, but maybe Clay Younger knows where he is.

He led the stallion over to a cottonwood tree and tied its reins to a low limb, battling the fiery rage making his temples pound, his heart labor. He strode across the road and walked to a set of sagging front steps, drawing his .44 as he reached for the door latch, a rawhide cord dangling from a hole in the wood planking.

With one swift jerk he pulled the latch string and kicked the door open, aiming his Colt into the shack's single room. A huge figure lay on a cot beside one window, apparently asleep.

Slocum crossed the floor quickly, just as Clay Younger raised his head off a greasy pillow to see who was there.

"Wake up, Clay," Slocum snarled, forcing the muzzle of his gun into Younger's open mouth. For added emphasis, he cocked the pistol and shoved it deeper between Clay's lips, farther down his throat.

Clay's eyes rounded. He looked down at the gun, blinking, then back to Slocum's face, his arms and legs stiffening.

"Don't move, Younger," Slocum warned, his voice barely above a whisper now. "It'll take a cleaning woman half a day to wash all your brains off that wall behind you. I'm gonna ask you some questions and unless I get straight answers, I swear I'll blow your goddamn head off."

Clay stared into his eyes, not blinking now. He gave a slight nod, moving his head just once.

"Your friend Lyle Sloan has a girl as his prisoner. Have you seen them?"

Clay wagged his head this time, then he tried to talk with Slocum's iron gun barrel filling his mouth.

Slocum pulled his Colt back a few inches until the muzzle rested against Clay's upper front teeth. "Tell me, Clay, and be real sure of your answer. If you lie to me, I'll come back and there won't be any questions. I'll just kill you, and you'll know why. Won't be no need for any explanation."

Clay's arms began to tremble. Very slowly, he lowered his head to the pillow. "You gotta be the craziest sumbitch I ever met," he said, sounding strangled and Slocum knew it was a result of the boot he'd planted in Younger's throat.

"No doubt about it," Slocum agreed, pressing his gun barrel a little harder against Clay's tobacco-stained teeth.

"I get plumb crazy mad when somebody crosses me. I killed your brother and I coulda killed you easy that night. I let you live, but I promise you I won't be so generous the next time. I've planted better men than you in graveyards all over the West. I lost track of the body count years ago. But you're gonna be next, unless you tell me everything you know."

"Jesus," Clay croaked, sweat beading on his forehead. "If Lyle finds out I talked, he'll kill me. I'm a dead man either way."

Slocum grinned savagely. "Not if I find Sloan first. He's gonna be buried right beside your brother the minute I find him, and you can take that to the bank."

He could see wheels turning in Younger's brain. "Lyle's faster'n you. Nobody's faster—"

"You'll never know," Slocum promised, his humorless grin fading, his mouth becoming a severe line across his face. "You won't be here to find out because I'm gonna decorate this wall with your brains unless you tell me what I want to know."

Clay swallowed hard. "I never talked to Lyle. He sent me word by a kid to come to Anna's place, that he had this girl tied to a bed an' we'd have some fun with her tonight. I tol' the kid to tell Lyle I wasn't feelin' too good on account of them kicks you gave me. My fuckin' ribs are so sore I can't hardly sit up in bed."

"Now you know how bad I hurt after you jumped me," Slocum told him. He thought about what Clay said, still holding his gun steady in front of Clay's lips. Myra was being held prisoner at a whorehouse named Anna's, tied to a bed, no doubt suffering torture and humiliation beyond comprehension. "Tell you what I'm gonna do, Clay. I'll tie you to this bed just like Sloan said he'd done to the woman. If you're telling the truth, I'll come back after I'm finished with him and I'll let you loose.

But if you're lying to me, when I come back it won't be to unfasten any ropes. I hope I've made that real clear."

"That's what the boy said," Clay pleaded, trying to control the quivering in his arms by gripping a soiled sheet underneath him.

Slocum straightened and took the gun away from Clay's mouth as he gave the little cabin a passing glance. Clay's pistol and gun belt were hanging from the back of a hide-bottom chair and a short-barreled shotgun rested in one corner of the room. "Lie real still," he said, turning back to Clay. "I'm gonna take your guns and tie you to the bed with a gag over your mouth. If you've told me the truth I'll come back and set you free, but I don't figure I need to tell you what I'm gonna do if Sloan and the girl aren't at Anna's."

With the gun muzzle away from his lips, Clay became more defiant. "Lyle's gonna kill you. You ain't near good enough to take him on an' I'll be stuck, tied to this goddamn bed."

"The rest will do you good," Slocum replied, walking over to the chair for the pistol, then to the corner for Clay's shotgun, thinking about the risks when he tied Younger to the bed, a chance for the big man to use his strength when Slocum needed both hands for the ropes. Even badly hurt, Clay would be dangerous. "I'll be back," he added, crossing over to the bed with the twelve gauge clamped in his left fist, covering Clay with his Colt .44.

He swung a sudden, vicious blow downward with twin barrels of the shotgun, cracking heavy iron across Clay's forehead with all the force he could muster. Younger wasn't prepared for the lick and was far too late trying to block the shotgun with his hands. His eyelids fluttered, then they closed and his entire body went slack.

"Sorry," Slocum whispered, heading for the door to fetch his lariat rope from the saddlehorn. "You'll have a little touch of headache when you wake up, but it won't kill you and I can't have you showing up, warning Sloan of what I have planned for him this evening."

He went down creaking steps and hurried across the darkening road to his horse, hanging Clay's pistol belt over his saddlehorn after he took down his lariat. Resting Clay's sawed-off shotgun against the cottonwood trunk, Slocum walked back to the shack and went inside.

He bound Clay hand and foot, lashing him to the bed with what remained of a forty-foot sisal he used when roping a stray cow. When he was satisfied with the knots he searched Clay's belongings and found an undershirt that could be fitted into a gag across Younger's mouth.

As darkness fell on Austin, Slocum made his way to his horse and loosened the reins, taking Clay's shotgun after a quick check of the loads. Both barrels held charges. If it came to a close-quarters fight with Lyle Sloan, the shotgun might come in handy.

He mounted painfully and looked west, in the direction of Anna's place. Slocum spoke to himself quietly as he nudged the bay with his heels.

"I'm headed your way, Sloan. Get ready to meet your Maker."

As he rode away from Clay's shack he spotted a woman in a plain cotton sack cloth dress watching him from her front porch. He tipped his hat to her, then he put his mind back on business.

17

Full darkness blanketed Sixth Street. The stud's horseshoes clicked over bricks in the road, pounding out a regular beat as Slocum rode toward Anna's. It was early for the whorehouse district and few people were about, allowing him to pass virtually unnoticed through a rough section of town to climb a hill where better-heeled clients sought their pleasures in finer surroundings. Only a few red conductor's lanterns had been lit above doorways at some of the smaller cribs. Slocum recalled a tale told by a railroader that many trainmen visited whores on longer runs and they marked the spots where women could be hired by hanging red lanterns on the right porches, so other train crews could find the same form of entertainment without asking local citizens in strange towns what to some might be an embarrassing question.

He sighted an older two-story house with peeling whitewash, sitting back from the road at the top of the hill. Just three or four downstairs windows were lit. A sunning porch ran around three sides of the house. A brick walkway led to steps near the front door.

"This has to be it," Slocum said under his breath, reining the stallion to a halt in front of the place while he examined it in darkness. An alley for trash wagons ran in back of the house and it would be typical of a whorehouse to have hitchrails in back so customers couldn't be identified by their horses tied out front. Most men were careful to hide proof of their lust from passersby, especially the hypocrites who sat in front pews at church on Sunday, offering "amens" to damnations of sinners who consorted with fallen women, handed down by some local preacher.

Slocum heeled the stud forward, riding to a dark street corner where he turned, heading for the mouth of an alleyway that would take him behind Anna's. Riding almost blind in deep night shadows, he freed his gun from its hammer thong and took his Greener shotgun from a rawhide string looped through the trigger guard.

His bay snorted, bowing its neck, then the big animal relaxed and continued toward a small stable where several horses were stalled. In the dark Slocum knew he would never recognize the horse Sloan rode—he hadn't taken a good look at it today up on the bluff, all his attention fixed on its rider.

He stopped the stud at a corner of the stable and swung down as quietly as he could, mildly irritated by the creak of saddle leather.

For a few moments he stood rock-still in the darkness with an ear cocked toward the house. Once, he thought he heard distant laughter coming from an upstairs window, although it ended too abruptly for him to be certain of the sound. Slocum counted five horses in the stable, and a row of saddles hung on top rails of horse stalls.

As he was about to begin a cautious approach toward a rear door, he heard hinges squeak. A broad-shouldered man carrying a lantern and a shotgun came out on the back stoop, holding his lamp high, peering into shadows around the barn.

"Who's there?" a gruff voice shouted.

Slocum had precious little time to think of a plan. "I'm a stranger," he called out, tying off the stud's reins, resting the shotgun against a stable wall. "Just passin' through town and I was told this was a nice place to find . . . a pretty girl."

"The girls ain't dressed fer the evenin' yet, mister. You got here too early."

Slocum walked slowly toward the lantern, ambling along like a man who wasn't quite sure of himself. He'd made a quick choice to pass himself off as a customer, thus to get inside without any shooting. The house was big and it would take time to locate the room where Sloan was most likely keeping Myra. "I sure wish you could make an exception," he said, lowering his voice when he neared the man on the rear stoop. "I've been travelin' for days and I sure do fancy a pretty woman. Price wouldn't be no object if the woman was pretty . . ."

"Come closer so I can see your face, stranger. We're real particular 'bout who we let inside. This ain't no bawdy house. We cater to gentlemen . . . don't allow no trash in here."

Slocum approached the circle of light spilling from the lantern. "As you can see by the cut of my clothes I'm not the sort who'd go to a bawdy house. I'm a businessman."

"What kinda business are you in?" the guard asked, still wary, cradling his double barrel shotgun in the crook of an arm like he expected trouble.

"Blooded horses," Slocum replied. "I've been buyin' up good Remount stock. Got a contract with the army in Colorado Territory to furnish thoroughbred cavalry horses. Been down looking at those Steeldust horses in Mexico."

He stopped when he was ten or twelve feet from the stoop so the guard could examine him, hoping their voices hadn't attracted the attention of Sloan or anyone else in an upstairs bedroom. Standing in the lantern's glow, Slocum made a perfect target for a shooter from a rear window.

"You look respectable enough, I reckon," the man said, "but I'll have to ask Miss Anna if she's got a girl ready this early in the evenin'." He chuckled. "Hell, maybe she'll see to you her own self. You're her type . . . . she likes men long an' lean."

"I'd be grateful if you made an inquiry for me," Slocum told him. "I'm a little on the randy side tonight. It's been quite a spell since I had a woman." It would be a tremendous piece of luck if he could be Anna's customer tonight. She would know which room Sloan was in.

"Must be," the guard remarked, making a half turn for the door, "to be out so damn early."

Slocum grinned. "A man's got natural desires. He can't always control 'em when they overtake him."

As the man was about to go back inside, he gave Slocum a second glance. "By the way, mister, Miss Anna don't allow no firearms inside. I can see you're packin' a pistol under that coat. If Anna lets you in, you'll have to check your gun at the door."

Slocum's heart sank. Facing a shootist like Sloan without his .44 wasn't to his liking. He had his .32 caliber bellygun hidden under his shirt. However, if the guard searched him thoroughly, he would find it. "I've got no problem with that," he said, making it sound casual. "I didn't come here to do any shootin'," he replied.

"Be back in a minute," the man said, pushing the door inward before going inside.

Thinking fast, Slocum tucked his .32 down into his undershorts so that it rested next to his cock. By clamping his legs together he'd be able to keep it from falling down his pants leg long enough to be searched.

Waiting in total darkness now, Slocum looked up at a row of rear windows, finding all of them dark. Somewhere in this house, probably in an upstairs bedroom, Myra was a prisoner being ravaged by a crazed, sadistic killer. Again, Slocum's blood began to boil as he thought about it. Unconsciously, his hands balled into fists at his sides.

Moments later the door opened and as a reflex, Slocum felt his muscles tense. If Sloan had glimpsed him from a window, he would be forced to make his play now.

A woman with flowing blonde tresses came out on the stoop, followed by the guard. She stared at Slocum in lamplight, then a slow smile crossed her face.

"I understand you're looking for a woman tonight," she said in a throaty voice. The front of her dressing gown hung open a bit, enough to give him a look at the cleft of pendulous breasts. "The price is four dollars, in advance. We don't do business with down-and-out cowboys or drifters who haven't got the price of an hour with a truly beautiful lady."

"Sounds plenty reasonable to me," he replied, holding his thighs together to keep his pistol from dropping down his pants leg.

"Another thing," she continued, noticing the bulge of a gun under his coat, "I don't allow firearms in my establishment. If you like what you see, I'll take you upstairs for an hour of good relaxation and excitement, but you'll have to check your pistol with Jory first."

Slocum opened his coat and drew his Colt, handing it up to Jory butt-first. "I only carry it for protection on the road during my travels," he explained, with as much sincerity as he could muster. "I haven't fired it for years, but the sight of it keeps most men honest. I reckon it's a good thing, too. I'm not much of a marksman with it. I'm a peace-loving man, but when I carry large sums of money I feel better with a gun."

Jory took the revolver. "You want me to search him, Miss Anna?"

Anna seemed to be looking at the bulge in the crotch of his pants now and it worried Slocum.

"That won't be necessary, Jory. I'm a good judge of character and this gentleman has an honest face." She smiled again. "A very handsome honest face at that." Anna spoke to Slocum. "Please come in. My name is Anna, and I promise you won't be disappointed when we get upstairs."

"I'm John," he said, returning her smile, starting for the steps while hoping he could keep the .32 in place. "Pleased to make your acquaintance."

She laughed. "Everybody who comes here is named John," she said. "But names don't matter anyway." She turned for the door and held it open for him as he crept up on the stoop. "All that matters is having a good time."

He walked past Jory into a rear foyer, reaching into a pants pocket for money. After being robbed by Clay he had less than ten dollars to his name. He made a flourish of counting out four bank notes while pausing near a hat rack. Slocum handed Anna the currency and removed his hat, placing it on a wall peg beside the door.

Anna folded the money and took his arm, giving him her best seductive smile. "Come with me," she said, tucking bills into a pocket of her pale blue dressing gown. "I think I'm really going to enjoy this. You look like you're one hell of a man underneath all those clothes."

Walking tight-legged with the bellygun trapped between his thighs, he followed her to a set of stairs leading to the second floor, pretending to admire oil paintings and other decorations in a dimly lit hallway leading to the staircase. "This is a very nice place you've got, probably the nicest I've seen this side of Denver."

"Nothing but the best for our good customers," she told him as he navigated the stairs awkwardly to keep the hidden gun in place. "You walk like you're stiff from too many hours in your saddle, John. When I get you on a mattress I'll rub your back and shoulders first, then a few other places. You've paid for an hour and I assure you you'll get your money's worth with me. I know how to make a man feel good all over. You'll see."

"I have no doubts about it," he said, holding onto a polished handrail. "You are a very beautiful woman and you seem to have an good understanding of men who aren't . . . quite comfortable coming to a place like this."

She nodded as they reached the top of the stairs, unaware when Slocum gave the upstairs hallway a cautious examination, half expecting to see Sloan coming in or out a bedroom door at a most inopportune time, his only weapon caught in his underclothing where he'd be too slow reaching for it.

"Most men with good breeding are quite bashful," she said, guiding him toward one end of the empty hall where a lone candle burned inside a glass globe on a small table between two bedroom doors. "You won't be shy with me after we have a glass of good sherry. I'll rub your sore muscles with scented oil and you'll be completely relaxed in no time."

They came to a door at the end of the hallway and Anna opened it with a key. Inside a spacious bedroom, a four-poster bed sat against one wall with a tiny oil lamp glowing softly on a nightstand beside it.

He walked in the room as Anna closed the door behind them, and at the same time he noticed a dressing screen in one corner. He'd been worried how to get his .32 out of his shorts without her seeing it and the screen offered him a perfect place to put on a show of bashfulness.

"Sit down on the edge of the bed, John," Anna said. "I'll pull off your boots. I can hang your coat from the hook behind the dressing screen."

He turned to her, feigning embarrassment. "If you don't mind I'd like to undress over yonder behind that screen, and I hope you'll understand if I ask you to turn out the lamp. I've always been kinda uneasy about taking off my clothes in front of a woman."

She grinned and pointed to the dressing screen. "Suit yourself, John, but I promise I'll get you over your shyness after a bit."

"Sorry to be this way," he muttered sheepishly, silently thankful for the opportunity he needed to put the .32 in one of his boots without being seen. "I was raised up in an old fashioned family."

He walked toward the screen when Anna's voice stopped him in mid stride. "That looks like a dangerous weapon you've got in your pants."

He glanced at her, feeling his pulse race. "What do you mean?" he asked, tensing slightly.

Anna was still smiling. "That big cock of yours. I can see how large it is by the lump in your pants. I'm glad you've already got a hard-on. Now hurry and get out of those clothes."

18

He secreted the bellygun in his right boot as Anna turned down the lamp. She left the wick glowing, casting faint light over her room, an expensive oriental rug, the lacy canopy above her bed, wallpaper dotted with prints of tiny pink flowers, a huge wardrobe cabinet, dressing table and mirror, a washstand with ceramic pitcher and bowl. Some sort of rose scent permeated the air, thick, assailing his nostrils while he undressed behind the screen. When he glanced over the top he found Anna staring at him from the bed, her gown down around her waist. Her bulbous breasts sagged from their own weight. She'd seen better days even though the years had been kind to her. Women in her profession often died young, of disease, opium addiction, a fondness for liquor, in Slocum's experience. Yet she was a beautiful woman, probably approaching her mid thirties, old for a woman in the sin trades.

He walked around the dressing screen, his cock enlarging when he got a closer look at her breasts. This wasn't the time for pleasure and he knew it, not with Myra being subjected to what Lyle Sloan had in mind if the story Clay told him was the truth. Somehow, Slocum had to get the information he needed without alerting Anna to his real purpose here tonight. But how was he to do it without playing out his part in the role he'd chosen for himself as a customer? For the time being, with Myra's safety in mind, he had no choice but to behave as a whorehouse visitor should while finding ways to ask about Sloan, and what room he might be in.

"You have beautiful breasts," he said, halting at the edge of the screen, torn now between lust and the need to rescue Myra as quickly as possible. Dancing light from the lamp's tiny flame revealed almost every detail of Anna's bosom.

Anna was eyeing his crotch. "God, what a dick you've got. It's one of the biggest I ever saw. Thick, too. You're sure to be a great lover with a dick like that. Come over here, John. Let me get a closer look at it . . ."

He stepped closer, still pretending to be shy about such matters. "I haven't had much experience," he lied, sounding as embarrassed as he could. All the while his mind was racing, to think of a way to ask about Myra or Sloan. The simplest and quickest way was to come clean and perhaps even threaten Anna with a gun to her head. But if things went wrong and she cried out for Jory, the guard downstairs, all hell would break loose and Myra could be in even more danger when Sloan heard shouts of alarm. He decided to continue to play along. He took a hesitant step foward, putting him within arm's reach of Anna, her earthy woman's scent making him wish he was just here for fun. She reached for his blood-engorged member, wrapping her dainty fingers around it.

"My goodness John, my fingers won't reach around

it. You're sure to be one of the best rides I've had in a long time."

Slocum took a deep breath, holding it in, trying to keep his mind on the business at hand not the hand on his cock. "Before we . . . get started, maybe you'll know the whereabouts of an old friend of mine from up in Fort Worth. Lyle Sloan is his name."

A tiny trace of concern wrinkled her brow. "How is it you know Lyle?" she asked, stroking Slocum's prick slowly, gently.

"I made his acquaintance a few years ago. I met him in the Hell's Half Acre district. Another acquaintance of mine may have some work for him. Lyle's a darn good pistoleer and my friend is having some trouble with a neighboring rancher over some stolen cattle. The neighbor hired a couple of gunslicks, but nobody's better'n Lyle with a pistol."

The worry left Anna's face. "I know Lyle," she said with a smile. "In fact, I can take you to him, but not now. Pleasure before business, John. I want to feel this huge dick inside me tonight. After we've had our fun, I'll show you where Lyle is."

In some measure Slocum was relieved, for Anna's remark was an indication that Sloan was here, at her place, just like Clay said he was. Now, all he could do was hope Myra hadn't suffered too much. "I'd be obliged," he said, unable to ignore his throbbing erection now. Anna would be suspicious if he asked to see Sloan before he made love to her.

Anna continued to jack his cock, admiring it in the small light cast by the lamp, a glassy look in her eyes. "I'm quite sure now," she said huskily. "This is the biggest dick I've ever seen. It's like a tree trunk. It'll be wonderful, trying to take it all inside me. I'm getting wet just thinking about it. Lie down, John. Lie down between my legs. I don't think I can wait any longer."

She opened the sash binding her gown and lay back across the mattress, completely naked underneath her garment. He knelt at the foot of the bed and crawled between her milky white thighs.

Anna seized his cock again, gripping it with a trembling hand, guiding it toward her glistening mound.

He resigned himself to the task and promised himself to make short work of it. Inching forward on his hands and knees, he put the head of his member between the moist lips of her cunt. "I've always had a problem with coming too quick," he whispered near her ear. "Maybe, after I talk to Lyle about my friend's problem I'll come back and pay for another hour."

Her breathing quickened and a soft moan escaped her lips. "I might not ask you to pay for a second hour," she sighed as she wrapped her legs around his buttocks, hunching against his stiff prick hungrily, grinding her pelvis to take the first few inches of it despite a tight fit. "Oh my goodness!" she gasped when he penetrated her. "That feels absolutely delightful! Give me more of it, my darling. I want it all—"

Slocum pushed another inch of thick cock into her pussy and felt her shudder underneath him.

"Suck my nipples," Anna whispered, thrusting her pussy back and forth on his shaft, straining to take more of his prick into her slick depths.

He cupped one massive fleshy breast in his hand and lifted her nipple to his lips, biting it gently at first before he took it deeper into his mouth, sucking harder, licking the end of her nipple with the tip of his tongue, feeling it twist into a ripe hard bud.

Anna groaned with pleasure, hunching faster, harder, while drawing him deeper with her heels, her fingers clamped around his buttocks. "This is so wonderful," she moaned. "Give me all of it . . . please!"

He drove the full length of his cock inside her and every muscle in her body went rigid, then she shook from head to toe and began hammering the lips of her cunt against the base of his shaft. Her fingernails dug into his flesh, ramming him toward her with all her strength. She rocked beneath him in a frenzy of lust and desire. Her mouth flew open and she started to pant frantically, as if she'd almost run out of air.

"Oh my darling!" she cried, rocking the bed with her passion as she neared a climax, her eyes tightly closed. "Faster! Do it faster!"

He granted her request and hunched furiously, feeling his balls rise, ready to explode, pushing thoughts of Myra from his mind for the moment, telling himself this was necessary to come to her rescue.

At the height of her thrusting she shrieked, rising up off the mattress with her spine, shuddering with the release of her fierce climax.

At almost the same instant Slocum gave in to sensations of pleasure and released his load, sending come in regular bursts into the bottom of her cunt, driving his cock hard and deep as his testicles emptied with the sound of her cries ringing in his ears.

Anna collapsed limply, wheezing through her nose and mouth when her passion was spent. Her legs relaxed. She released her powerful grip on his ass and lay perfectly still, sucking air into her lungs.

He lay atop her, drawing his own quick breaths as the last of his jism leaked into her pussy. For a time he remained still and said nothing, gazing down at Anna's closed eyes.

Then her eyelids fluttered. "I thought the world had come to an end," she gasped, her chest heaving. "I haven't had one like that in years . . . I was sure I was going to faint. You won't ever have to pay for another visit to my bedroom, darling John. From now on, everything's on the house."

Slocum forced his mind back on the business that brought him here. "Maybe, after I talk to Lyle, we can do this again," he said quietly, pulling a grin. "I promised my rancher friend I'd offer Lyle a proposition."

Anna stared past him to the canopy above her bed. "I'm just too weak to show you to his room. He's right here down the hall, in room number nine."

Slocum pushed up on his elbows, slowly withdrawing his limp prick from her dripping pussy. "I'll get dressed and go tap on his door. As soon as we're done with our business discussion, I'll come back and we'll start all over again. Don't bother with getting dressed. I shouldn't be very long."

Her expression told him she'd remembered something. "He's got a girl with him . . . some sort of misunderstanding between two lovers, I think. If you know Lyle then you know he can be kinda rough on his women sometimes. He carried her up to the room and I saw some blood on her face. He told me she got drunk and she passed out. Lyle's a good customer, so I told him he could use the room for a couple of days until they got their misunderstanding straightened out."

"Yeah, that's Lyle all right," Slocum said as he got off the bed to dress, hiding the anger in his voice when he heard about Myra's condition. "He never did have much respect for a woman, if I remember right."

He went behind the screen and dressed, tucking the .32 in his waistband, covering it with his shirt before he pulled on his boots. "I won't be long," he said, walking softly to the door to let himself out. Slocum forced another grin as he glanced over his shoulder. "Wait right here for me, pretty lady. The next time, I promise I'll make it more exciting."

"I don't know how much more exitement I can stand," Anna purred as he twisted the doorknob. "Another dose of that big dick could kill me."

Slocum smiled and closed the door behind him, all thoughts of pleasure erased from his brain. In light from the single candle he read a number above Anna's doorway, number one.

Sloan is at the other end of the hall, he thought.

Creeping forward on the balls of his feet, he tugged his shirt tail from his pants and took out his Colt New Line .32, a pocket model with no trigger guard, making it easier to conceal under his clothing. The little gun could be deadly at close range, if its owner's aim was true. Slocum judged he would have very little time from the moment he kicked the door in until a well-placed shot was needed, and he'd probably have to find his target in the dark. Of just as much importance he had to be sure his bullet missed Myra. But would he have enough time to make that choice?

He passed soundlessly down the hallway, reading room numbers as he went, worrying that a creaking floorboard in an old house might give him away, alerting Sloan to his approach, allowing an experienced gunman to be ready.

He recalled what Anna said, about seeing blood on Myra's face, that she was unconscious when Sloan brought her here. He knew she hadn't passed out from drinking—Sloan had beaten her unconscious.

"I'll have to kill him," Slocum whispered. "He won't have it any other way." He never considered things might work out differently, that it would be John Slocum's name carved on a tombstone. He would be leaving two bodies buried in Austin after he left. It was true, what he'd told Clay earlier, that he'd stopped counting bodies a long time ago.

As he feared it might, a floorboard squeaked softly as he crossed it and the sound made him flinch. He stopped and cocked an ear toward the end of the hall to listen for stirring in any of the rooms.

When all was quiet, save for the murmur of voices downstairs, he continued slow steps onward, passing the candle in its smudged glass globe, then the threshold at the top of the stairs. His boots made no noise while he made his way toward the far end of the hallway.

Slocum crept past doors marked five and six, and by the way numbers were arranged he spotted the door to number nine long before he got there. His grip tightened on the butt of his .32 and he noticed his breathing was shallow.

"You rotten bitch!"

A muffled voice from number nine halted him in his tracks, a deep, angry voice.

A slapping sound, hard to hear behind a closed door, sent Slocum forward again, gritting his teeth with rage.

A soft woman's cry followed, like something was tied over her mouth.

"That's it, you son of a bitch!" Slocum hissed, spotting a faint light coming under the door. Sloan had a lantern lit and that was exactly what Slocum was hoping for.

"I'll be able to see you when I kill you, you bastard," he said.

Slocum drew in a breath. A savage countenance changed his expression. It was time to square accounts with Lyle Sloan for the beating he'd given Myra.

19

Slocum threw his shoulder into the door, well aware of
what it would do to his sore ribs. The doorjam splintered
where the latch plate was afixed and in a split second
he found himself in a small bedroom, standing with his
feet planted, the bellygun in his fist.

A shape whirled away from the bed, a tall man in a
white shirt and suspenders, dark pants tucked into stovepipe boots, a gunbelt buckled around his waist. A naked
girl was tied to the head and foot bedposts, her face
swollen and purple in light from an oil lamp glowing on
a dresser across the room.

Slocum drew dead aim on his adversary, the man he
knew had to be Lyle Sloan . . . Sloan was clawing for
his gun.

"Go for it!" Slocum roared, his anger unleashed when
he saw the condition Myra was in. "Grab that piece and
I'll end it now!"

Sloan was clearly taken by surprise. His hand froze
above the butt of his pistol. "How the hell did you get
in here, you son of a bitch.?"

"It doesn't matter how," Slocum snarled, hoping the

crack of the doorjam and his shout wouldn't bring Jory or anyone else upstairs until he was finished with the lesson he planned to give Sloan.

Sloan stared at Slocum with the palest gray eyes he had ever seen, almost catlike orbs in the glow from the lantern. For a moment Sloan stood still, half turned from the bed where Myra lay in rope bindings. "You gotta be that guy Slocum," he said in a chilly voice matching his icy eyes.

"I won't waste time with proper introductions," Slocum told him evenly. "All you need to know is that I'm here to make you pay for what you did to this woman. You're a cowardly son of a bitch. I'm gonna hurt you for what you did to Myra and before I hurt you, I wanted you to know why. Cowards like you disgust me. This state's gonna be a better place without you. Get a good look at me, Sloan. Get a close look at the man who's gonna watch you draw your last breath unless you do exactly what I tell you."

Sloan glanced at Slocum's revolver. "That little pea-shooter may not do it, Slocum. I'm packin' a forty-four, an' unless you are real good with a gun, I'll take you down, even if you get off the first shot."

Slocum acknowledged the threat with a nod. "I've taken all that into consideration and I'm willing to take the chance. Go for your pistol. This conversation's running longer than it needs to."

"You're bluffin'. You won't gun me down in cold blood. It ain't no easy thing, killin' a man."

Slocum moved to one side of the doorframe to keep anyone from slipping up behind him. "I've had lots of practice killing men. You're right about it not being easy, but sometimes it's necessary. Unless you raise those hands high above your head and walk in front of the gun down to the sheriff's office, I'll demonstrate just how easy it is for me to kill a no-good yellow son of a bitch who'd beat a woman."

Sloan made no move to lift his palms. He glared at Slocum with hatred twisting his face. "You ain't got no idea how dumb you are," he croaked, a barely noticeable curling in the fingers of his gun hand.

Slocum cocked his bellygun, aiming carefully, his hand as steady as a rock. "Go ahead, reach for it," Slocum said very softly. "I'll show you which one of us is dumb."

The gunman's arrogance wouldn't allow this last remark and his hand dipped lightning-fast for his pistol. Slocum turned his aim just a fraction wide and pulled the trigger.

The little Colt barked, cracking in his fist. A ball of lead was propelled by a finger of bright flame into Lyle Sloan's right shoulder, exiting through the back of his shirt along with a tiny spray of blood and soft tissue splattering on the wallpaper behind him. Force of impact swung Sloan around, bending him double with sudden pain.

Myra screamed, her cry smothered by a scarf tied over her mouth.

At the same time Slocum lunged, grabbing Sloan's holstered pistol, jerking it free before he stepped back out of reach of a fist or a hidden knife. Sloan groaned, but he did not go down to the floor.

"What the hell was that noise?" a voice cried from downstairs. "Sounded like a gun . . ."

Slocum ignored everything else. He tucked his smoking .32 into his belt and turned Sloan's own revolver toward him as he thumbed back the hammer. "Now," Slocum said savagely, his lips drawn tight across his teeth. "If you can reach your ass with your lips, bend over and kiss it good-bye."

"Good-bye?" Sloan mouthed the word, and despite his pain and surprise, his eyebrows lifted when he asked the question.

Slocum heard rapid footsteps coming up the stairs. "Kiss your ass good-bye," he said again, aiming the .44 at Sloan's head while he moved around behind him. "A son of a bitch like you doesn't deserve to breathe the same air the rest of us are breathin'. I've killed a lot of men, but I've never executed an unarmed man. So in your case, I'm gonna make an exception. I aim to give you a chance." He tossed his .32 on the bed in front of Sloan. "Reach for it, you yellow bastard. I'll give you a chance to pick it up and turn around."

He seized Sloan by the back of his shirt collar and shoved him roughly toward the bed, placing the muzzle of the Colt at the base of Sloan's skull.

Sloan dove for Slocum's bellygun. Slocum waited until Sloan had it fisted. As Sloan was wheeling around, Slocum pulled the trigger on Sloan's .44.

Slocum's bullet hit Sloan in his left eyesocket, knocking him back against the bedroom's windowpane. Blood squirted over the wall as Sloan fell backward, shattering through the pane of glass as he tumbled out the second story window.

Heavy boots clomped down the hallway in Slocum's direction, but the sounds were not loud enough to prevent him from hearing Sloan thud to the dirt below, abruptly ending his scream. Only then did Slocum whirl toward the doorway, leveling the .44 at whoever was headed to room number Nine.

Jory stumbled to a halt in the doorframe holding his shotgun in both hands.

"Drop it!" Slocum ordered, aiming squarely at Jory's chest. "Mr. Sloan jumped out the window. If he's still alive you might want to send for a doctor. I imagine he's busted up real bad."

"He jumped?" Jory asked, bewildered by what he'd just heard, looking past Slocum at the remnants of window glass clinging to the frame. "I coulda swore I heard two gunshots—"

"Probably just breaking glass. It all took place so fast I couldn't tell you just how it happened."

"But why would he jump? That don't make a lick of sense."

Slocum shrugged, still covering Jory with the pistol. "He took one look at me and ran across the room like he'd seen a ghost. I reckon he must have forgotten he was two floors high when he did it."

Jory's expression turned doubtful. "Where'd you get the gun? I disarmed you downstairs a while ago."

"This one belongs to Mr. Sloan. Far as I know, this is the only gun there was."

Jory wasn't so easily swayed. "I figure maybe you pushed him out that window, mister." He continued to grip his scattergun, though the barrels were aimed at the floor.

"There's almost always two sides to any story," Slocum said casually, as if he were disussing the weather. "Why don't you go down there and ask him how it happened, if he can still talk. And while you're downstairs, send for the sheriff and a doctor for this girl. As you can see, Sloan gave her one hell of a beating tonight and she may have some serious injuries. She'll want to file charges against Sloan . . . if he's still alive. Might be all he'll need is an undertaker."

Anna appeared suddenly behind Jory, peering into the room clad in her dressing gown. "What the hell happened here?" she asked, examining Myra first, then the shattered windowpane.

"Seems Mr. Sloan did this girl a lot of harm, Anna," he began. "As you can see, she's tied to the bed and her face is one hell of a mess. Appears he hurt her pretty bad."

"Where's Lyle?" she asked. "Did he climb out my window?"

Slocum had trouble disguising a grin. "I wouldn't call it climbing out," he replied. "He sorta jumped."

"I'm sure I heard a gun," she said, looking from Slocum to the window again.

"It all happened so quick," he told her. "Maybe this gun did go off accidentally when he crossed this room so fast. I think you oughta send for the sheriff and a doctor. This girl looks like she needs medical attention."

"I can't guess why Lyle would jump," Anna muttered, then she hurried around Jory to the bed, examining Myra, beginning to untie her ropes and the gag over her mouth. "Go fetch Doc Hardin right away, Jory. This girl has received awful treatment, worse than anything Lyle's ever done before." She gave Slocum a look. "I know damn well I heard a couple of gunshots."

"I can't say for sure," Slocum lied, placing Sloan's pistol on the nightstand. "It happened real fast. Sloan tried to jump me an' then there was this real loud noise."

"What do I do about Lyle?" Jory asked, turning to go down the hall.

Anna aimed an angry look at Jory. "Let the bastard lie out there, for all I care. I won't tolerate this, not even from my best customers."

Jory hurried off, boots thumping on floorboards, then the stairs.

Slocum was thinking about what Anna said, that Sloan had beaten women before.

"Oh John," Myra stammered, tears streaming from her swollen eyes. "I was sure he was going to kill me—"

"Just lie quiet," Anna whispered to her. "The doctor will be here shortly. I've got some salve for your cuts and bruises. I'll go get them." She left the bed and went out, leaving Myra and Slocum alone.

He crossed over to the bed and touched her arm. Bleeding cuts leaked onto the sheet where ropes had been tied around her wrists and ankles. "Sorry I let this happen," he said gently, sincerely. "I should never have left you alone at the spring like I did."

Myra wiped tears from her face gingerly before she began covering her nakedness with a top sheet. "It's okay, John. I know you were only tryin' to protect me." She glanced over to the window. "I saw what really happened, you know. It didn't happen like you said, only I won't ever say a word to nobody. He got just what he deserved . . . he hurt me so bad I thought I was gonna die."

"I'll tell Sheriff Myers the truth, if he asks. Myers is the type who'll be glad to get rid of Sloan, if I'm any judge of things. Lyle Sloan was one of his problems that just went away. I don't expect any charges to be filed against me, but if it comes to that, you can tell a judge you saw Sloan reach for the gun I tossed on this bed, which is the truth."

"I know," Myra whispered. "I was so afraid he would kill you on account of he's so terrible mean."

"Some of the meanness just went out of him, I reckon," he said. "If he's still alive, he'll be busted up pretty bad and he won't be a threat to you or anybody. I'll go downstairs as soon as Anna gets back, to see if he's still breathing. I put a slug through his skull and don't many men outlive that."

"I love you, John," Myra told him. "I know you'll leave Austin pretty soon, because that's the kind of man you are. But I want you to know I'll still love you."

He grinned and made a move for the door when he heard Anna's footsteps. "Who knows?" he said to her. "Could be that when I'm ready to settle down, I'll come back and look you up if you haven't found another man by then."

Anna rushed into the bedroom. "You poor girl," she said, opening a jar of pungent ointment while she sat on the edge of the mattress, beginning to apply medicine gently to Myra's bleeding wrists and face. "I knew Lyle got a little rough with some of my girls, but never anything like this."

Slocum walked out, holstering Sloan's .44 until he found his own gun downstairs. A Peacemaker wasn't to his liking, lacking the proper balance he demanded from a sidearm.

At the bottom of the stairs he went to the back door and got his Colt from a shelf below his hat with half a dozen of Anna's girls watching him, then he walked outside and made a turn for the side window where Sloan had fallen.

He found the gunman lying on his back staring up at a sky full of twinkling stars with one good eye. He noticed Sloan take a shallow breath, a hollow sound. Learning Sloan was still alive somehow angered Slocum.

He stood over Sloan, blocking out light from the stars when his shadow fell on Sloan's face. "Sorry to see you're still breathin'," Slocum said. "Maybe it's a condition that won't last much longer. That's one hell of a hole in your face."

"You . . . bastard," Sloan croaked.

"Too bad. While you're waitin' for the doctor, think about what you did to Myra Reed. Think about how she felt, tied to a bed, knocked half senseless by a yellow son of a bitch who calls himself a man. Try to recall the way she screamed when your fist landed on her face. And then I want you to remember what it was like to dive out that window up yonder with a hole through your goddamn skull, the ground rushing up toward you fast as can be, until you came to this real sudden stop. Think about how it felt to stop so quick, with bones crackin' in your back. If you live, you'll be a half-blind cripple the rest of your life."

"You'd . . . better hope . . . I die, Slocum. I'll come . . . gunnin' for you."

Slocum drew his Colt and aimed down at Sloan's forehead. "I can put that worry behind me right now, Lyle," he said, then he laughed and wagged his head. "Maybe justice is better served if you live a while longer. As to the part about you ever gunning for me, I can promise you this . . . I'll be lookin' forward to it."

He lowered his pistol and turned away to check on his horse before the doctor and the sheriff arrived.

20

His horse stood quietly, head lowered in the darkness, when he arrived at the stable behind Anna's. Slocum's anger cooled while he rubbed the stud's neck, feeling drained. He'd taken one hell of a chance going after Sloan the way he did and as he stood there, thinking about it now, he resolved to make a more determined effort to stay clear of trouble, no matter what. It seemed women got him in most of his fixes. If he'd only ridden on after that first night in Austin he wouldn't have sore ribs, bumps on his head, nor would he have had three men out to kill him. But when he remembered that first night with Myra, another side of him was thankful to have known a woman like her in bed. All in all, he supposed the rewards had been worth the dangers. Still, he was mighty glad his difficulties were over now.

He merely glanced at the Greener shotgun resting against the stable wall before returning to the back door of the house. It would be an ugly weapon in close-quarters fighting with eight-inch barrels, shredding everything it its path, requiring almost no aim on the part of its owner. The fact of the matter was that neither

Clay Younger nor his dead brother had turned out to be all that hard to handle. Bob had been downright foolish. Clay, on the other hand, was merely strong and very careless, making Slocum ponder how a man like him had survived the war. And Lyle Sloan was no great shakes when it came down to cases. He'd let Slocum get the drop on him tonight, all because of a woman. Slocum decided women were ultimately every man's downfall, one way or another. He counted himself lucky in that regard, since women had occupied so much of his adult life.

As he climbed the rear steps to the stoop he heard a horse trot into the alley. "That'll be the doctor," he said, going inside to visit Myra before he collected his gear at the hotel so he could leave town at first light.

Some of Anna's girls standing in the foyer fell silent when he walked in, staring at him, fearful of him he supposed after they learned what had happened upstairs. One particular redhead appealed to him, wearing a low-cut evening dress with silk stockings and high heel button shoes.

"Good evening, ladies," he said politely, tipping his hat as he walked toward the staircase. "Don't worry. All the excitement's over now. Tell the doctor to come up to room nine when he gets to the house. I think I heard him riding up just now."

The redhead gave him a puzzled look. "Doc Hardin drives a buggy, mister. Maybe that was Jory you heard . . ."

Slocum started up the stairs two at a time. "Jory can tell the doctor where the girl is," he replied.

At the top of the stairway he turned for the room where Myra was. A light beamed from the open door into room number nine. He meant to say good-bye to her in private if he could. He owed her that much, to bid her farewell in a personal way.

When he came in the room he found Anna ministering to the girl's cuts with salve and a cloth. "How is she?" he asked as he walked over to the bed.

"She'll be okay," Anna replied. She gave Slocum a wry smile. "I didn't know until now that the two of you knew each other. She just told me about you, about how much she loved you and wished you were staying in town."

Myra was watching him from a pile of pillows. "Miss Anna said she wanted you to stay, too," Myra said, "that you seemed like a real nice person even though she didn't know you hardly at all."

It was clear Anna hadn't told her about the time he spent in Anna's room earlier. He gave Anna a nod. "I wish I could stay, but I've got business farther north and it can't wait. If I could, I'd spend more time here."

Anna spoke to him, lowering her voice. "How about Lyle?" she asked. "Is he—"

"He's still alive. I figure his back's broken an' something's wrong with one of his eyes. He won't be giving nobody any trouble."

"The bastard had it comin'," Anna said darkly. "Look what he did to this girl's face."

Slocum looked at Myra. "I hope you'll be okay real soon," he told her. "I was afraid he'd already—" A commotion downstairs silenced Slocum, the sound of breaking glass and then several women screaming.

He whirled away from the bed, bewildered by the noises until he heard a bellowing roar from the ground floor.

"Where the hell's John Slocum?"

He recognized Clay's voice immediately. He'd been so sure of those knots he tied in the rope, doubling them because of Clay's size and strength. "It's Clay Younger," he said, jerking his Colt free. "Somebody untied him. Damn!"

Slocum crossed over to the doorway in two quick strides as more screams echoed from downstairs.

"Tell me where he is, you bitch!" Clay roared, just when Slocum entered the hallway.

"There's some stranger upstairs," a girl cried. "Nobody told us his name—"

Heavy boots thumped to the bottom of the staircase. Slocum ran toward the top of the stairway, hell-bent on stopping the older Younger from getting to the second floor, dead-sure Clay wouldn't have come here without a gun. In a flash Slocum remembered a woman watching him leave Clay's shack from a cabin porch across the road and instinct told him this was the person who had set Younger free.

Slocum reached the landing just as Clay started up and he aimed down with his pistol, briefly glimpsing twin barrels of a shotgun aimed up at him before a thundering blast shook the walls of Anna's house. The concussion reminded Slocum of cannon fire. He dove for the floor while seeing he'd been momentarily spared by the hand of fate—in Clay's haste he had tripped over one of the steps and triggered off a shotgun blast into the handrail and a wall beyond it. Splintering wood and bits of pellet-shredded wallpaper swirled in every direction as Clay struggled to regain his balance. It was all the time Slocum needed.

He fired at Clay's snarling face. Above the shotgun's roar Slocum heard a distinctive crack. Clay's jaw flew open and his backbone straightened from a crouch until he jerked erect with both feet planted on the stairs, bringing his shotgun up to fire its second charge. More shrill screams came from the downstairs foyer.

In a curious type of slow motion, Clay's forehead changed shape. Like a ripe pumpkin fallen off a wagon, the front and top of his head opened, splitting apart, halting Slocum's trigger finger when he was about to take another shot. A plug of twisted hair and scalp dropped away from Clay's skull and it seemed his eyes were being pushed through his head.

Slocum's ears were still ringing when Clay groaned, a sound barely audible in the aftermath of a tremendous explosion trapped in a small space. Amazingly, even at a short distance of less than twenty feet, Slocum's .44 caliber slug had not taken Clay off his feet when it struck the center of his forehead, passing through his brain, fracturing the front and back of his skull.

He's tough, Slocum thought, poised to fire again in spite of the obvious . . . Clay was as good as dead.

Bits of pulverized wood from the wall and handrail fell to the floor below and yet Clay still stood upright, clinging fast to his shotgun while blood cascaded down his face and neck in a grisly torrent, dribbling on his shirt, bloody droplets clinging to whisker stubble on his jaw and chin.

Seconds later, Clay tried to speak, yet his mouth was full of blood and only gurgling noises came from his lips. He swayed and righted himself. Time stood still for Slocum while he looked down at Clay

"You shoulda stayed where I put you," Slocum whispered. "Whoever untied you just got you killed."

"Dear God!" a woman's voice gasped behind him. Anna had peered around the corner at the top of the landing, and when she saw Clay's bleeding head, her hand flew to her mouth.

At long last Clay teetered, letting go of his shotgun. He coughed a mouthful of blood and sank to his knees, reaching for his skull. But when he knelt he lost his balance completely and tilted away from the wall, to the spot where the handrail might have kept him from falling, had it not been blown to bits by his first load of buckshot.

Like a mortally wounded grizzly Clay toppled off the staircase head-first, his huge hands clamped around his damaged face while he dropped to the floor downstairs, landing with a resounding thud.

Another chorus of screams came from the foyer the moment Clay fell. One girl began sobbing uncontrollably. Above the din Slocum heard Anna say, "How horrible. How ghastly. Dear God!"

Slocum came to his hands and knees, then his feet. "I know it wasn't a very pretty sight," he told her, holstering his .44 before he turned to Anna. "In case you didn't know him, he was one of Lyle's associates, so I was told. I had to kill his brother the other night when he came at me with a shotgun. I damn sure didn't ask for any of this, but the three of 'em would not have it any other way. Sorry about the mess I made here tonight. These gents just wouldn't leave it alone."

Anna nodded, her face as pale as talcum powder while she continued to stare at the damaged handrail where Clay had fallen moments ago. "I knew all about the Younger brothers. They'd turned the Steamboat into a slaughter house. It became a hangout for saddle tramps and loafers. Decent folks were scared to go in there."

The screaming stopped downstairs, only a lone girl's voice sobbing quietly now. Slocum spoke to Anna. "Please see to Myra and I'll drag that body out back until the doctor and the sheriff get here. I'll have some explaining to do to Sheriff Myers."

Anna made a face. "He's a spineless wonder. If he has any sense he'll thank you for what you did, cleaing up our town when it was his job."

Slocum wasn't so sure, but he started downstairs without a word about it for now. Men like Sheriff Myers sometimes got a bit cocky when all the dust from a fight settled.

He walked over to Clay's corpse and grabbed one of his arms to pull him across the floor, leaving a smear of blood behind him all the way to the back door. As he was going out he heard soft footfalls coming toward the rear of the house. When he looked out he recognized Dr. Hardin in lamplight spilling from the open doorway.

"Good grief," the doctor said when he got a look at Clay. "It's obviously too late to do anything for him—"

"There's a girl upstairs in room number nine who needs your attention, Doc," he said. "She took a pretty bad beating today and I hope she's okay."

"I'll examine her," Hardin said, stepping around the bulk of Clay's lifeless body to go inside.

Slocum spoke over his shoulder before he dragged Clay down the steps. "When you get done with the girl, there's a gent who went out a second story window around on the south side of the house. He claims his back's broken, an' he may have trouble seein' out of one eye. He's the sumbitch who beat up the girl, so you don't have to get in no hurry on my account when it's time to look at him."

"He fell out an upstairs window?" Hardin asked, pausing a few feet inside the foyer.

Slocum intended no humor when he replied, "He may have had a little help." Slocum pulled Clay off the stoop into the darkness just as Jory rode up to the stable in the alley.

Jory ran toward the house after his horse was tied, and when he saw the body with Slocum standing over it, he stumbled to a halt, gazing down for a moment, trying to see who it was in the shadows of night around them. "That's Clay Younger," Jory said, an almost reverent tone in his voice. "What the hell happened to his head?"

"I put a hole through it," Slocum answered. "He came at me with a shotgun on the stairs."

"Jesus!" Jory whispered, examining the corpse again before he looked up at Slocum. "I don't know who you are, mister, but you gotta be one bad *hombre*, whatever handle you go by. I done heard from Sheriff Myers that you killed Clay's brother an' then you went an' throwed the meanest son of a bitch who ever shit between a pair of boots plumb through a goddamn second floor window. I know you shot him first because I smelled gunsmoke in that room. Now you've gone an' blowed Clay Younger's head all to pieces. I can't figure how you done all this by yourself."

"Very carefully," Slocum said. "I reckon I had a fair share of good luck."

"Takes more'n luck," Jory remarked, like he knew all about these things. "It takes a man who knows how to kill folks."

"That really isn't my line of work," Slocum explained. "It just happened this way. They crossed me. I make a habit out of minding my own business, usually."

Jory was reading his face as best he could in light from the heavens at night. "I'd sure be proud to know your name, mister, if you wouldn't take no offense."

"No offense," he said, looking forward to a good night's sleep before he pulled out tomorrow. "I'm John Slocum and I'm most often in the horse business. Killing men who get in my way is just a sideline . . ."

21

He lay soaking in a high-backed iron bathtub at the Driskell bath house smoking a cheroot, drinking sour mash whiskey from the fresh bottle he bought on his way back from the Capitol Cafe, when he heard footsteps. As a precaution he placed the bottle on the floor and picked up his .32 from a chair where his clean duds were folded. Slocum had been enjoying hot soapy water and time to relax, and the possibility of a disturbance annoyed him. He watched the door, prepared for almost anything after the previous deadly sequence of events in Austin.

Sheriff John Myers walked in. He saw Slocum's pistol and for a moment there was a trace of fear in his eyes. "You won't shoot me, will you?" he asked, only half joking by the sound of his squeaky voice.

Slocum lowered his gun. "I guess you want some answers," he said, putting his pistol back on the chair.

Myers edged a little closer to the tub. "Just somethin' for the official record, Mr. Slocum, so I can tell the judge how it all happened. No need to tell me again about Bob. I talked to a kid who cleans spittoons at the Steamboat, a boy who works for ol' man Cobbs at the livery after school. He told me exactly how it happened, an' when the kid started talkin', a couple others said the same thing, that Bob come at you with a shotgun. I just came back from talkin' to Anna. She an' Jory Winters told me what they knew about what happened at her place. I tried to question Lyle Sloan, only he's unconscious over at the hospital now. Doc Hardin said he's probably gonna die from that bullet hole through his head. I know just about all I need to know when it comes to how you shot Clay. There was a whole house full of witnesses at Anna's. He came after you up them stairs an' he fired first, so it's plain an' simple self-defense. What nobody's all that clear on is what happened to Sloan. The girl, Myra Reed, keeps on sayin' how he fell out that window when you busted in the room, an' how he shot himself in the eye accidental. She told me how he tied her up an' beat her real bad, an' she's got the scars to prove it. But what don't make any sense at all is why a dangerous gunman like Sloan would fall out a window soon as he set eyes on you, an' shoot himself in the eye while he was at it. I wanted to hear your side of the story."

Slocum inhaled deeply on his cigar, blowing smoke toward the ceiling in lazy swirls. "Does it really matter, Sheriff?" he asked, disliking Myers too much to spend much time correcting Myra's version of events. "I busted down the door and saw the girl tied to the bed. After that, things happened so fast I'm having trouble remembering all the details. Maybe his gun went off when he went for it."

The sheriff seemed nervous now. His eyes flickered around the room as though he was unable to look directly at Slocum for his next question. "Sloan had a bullet hole in his shoulder, too. I can't see but one way he got that wound. You shot him, didn't you? You shot him down in cold blood."

Slocum shook his head in frustration. "That's what everybody said happened the night I shot Bob Younger, until that boy came forward with the truth."

"It's just for the record," Myers protested, lifting his hands.

Slocum fisted his whiskey again and took a mouthful before he said any more. "Then let me set the record straight for you, Sheriff. Lyle Sloan was a cowardly son of a bitch. He beat that girl within an inch of her life, while she was tied to bedposts. I found out where he was keeping her and I went to Anna's place. I found out which room they were in. I broke open the door and went in with a gun drawn on Sloan, only the damn fool thought he was faster. He went for his pistol and I shot him through the shoulder, so he'd be alive to stand trial for what he did to Miss Reed. But Sloan wouldn't let it go with that, and there was a scuffle. Somehow he wound up with a bullet in his eyesocket over by the window."

Myers cleared his throat. "The girl swears you didn't push him out . . . that he jumped, or maybe he fell. She said she had her eyes closed on account of how scared she was. What still don't make sense is that Jory said he searched you, an' took the gun you was carryin'. I don't reckon it matters all that much, since it was Sloan. This whole town'll be glad to be rid of him an' them Younger boys."

"Why not let it go at that?" Slocum asked, taking another swallow of whiskey. "If Sloan lives long enough to tell a different version of the story, it'll be my word against his, seeing as how Miss Reed says she had her eyes closed."

The sheriff nodded. "I hope you understand it's my job to question all the parties involved."

Slocum was suddenly angry. "If you'd been doing your job in the first place, men like Sloan and the Youngers wouldn't have been able to ride roughshod over folks in Austin. They'd be behind bars, where they belonged."

Myers spread his palms in a helpless gesture. "I already tried to explain to you that nobody'd back me up. I couldn't be expected to take 'em on single-handed, not men with that kind of reputation."

"Maybe there's a lesson in this for you, Sheriff," Slocum said, gazing thoughtfully at the ceiling. "Bad reputations don't necessarily make men tough. As far as I'm concerned, those three boys hadn't earned the right to make men afraid of 'em. It was mostly just tough talk . . . a hell of a lot of bluff."

"But they killed men right here in Austin," Myers protested, "like Tucker, an' he was god-awful mean with a gun."

"Sloan hand-picked his victims," Slocum suggested. "By all accounts, Tucker was dead drunk when he tangled with Sloan. It made a good story, only it seems to me it was just a couple of drunks going at each other with pistols over a card game. In my book, that don't make either one of 'em smart or tough. Stupid, is what I'd call it."

Myers cast a glance over his shoulder at the door. "I'd guess that's enough for my report to the judge an' the county attorney. Like you said, with no other witnesses it's just your word against that of Red Sloan, if he lives, an' his reputation won't get him much consideration."

Myers turned to leave, hesitating with a dash of color in his cheeks now. "Just between you an' me, Mr. Slocum, I'm mighty damn glad things turned out like they did. I am sure you understand why. The streets of Austin will be a helluva lot safer now."

Slocum's eyebrows knitted. "Frankly, I don't recall getting much help from you. That kid who works for Mr. Cobbs was a help."

The sheriff's face became deep red with embarrassment. "I suppose you'll be leavin' town tomorrow?" he asked before he left.

"Can't hardly wait to get back on the trail," Slocum replied honestly. He had only one regret. He would miss seeing Myra, and miss her wonderful, passionate cries during the night.

Slocum entered Myra's hospital room as dawn's early light beamed into her room from a window. He'd spoken with a nurse who told him Myra had minor internal injuries and she would only need a few days of rest. Crossing over to the bed, he smiled at her and got a warm smile in return, before her expression changed to sorrow.

"You're leavin', aren't you?" she asked.

He nodded once. "Business. I wish I could stay, but it simply isn't possible."

She reached for his hand and held it tightly. "I meant what I said, John, about lovin' you. I hope someday you'll come back to see me. Maybe things will be different."

"When I'm back this way I promise I'll look you up first thing."

"I'll still love you," she whispered, fighting back a swell of tears.

There was nothing else to be said. He bent down and kissed her swollen lips lightly. She wrapped one arm around his neck and held him for a short while, then she let him go.

"I'll remember the night we spent together for a long time," she said, searching his face. "Maybe for the rest of my life."

"I'm not likely to forget it either," he told her, backing away, turning for the door. "Good-bye, pretty lady. Take care of yourself."

Slocum left her room, pausing at another door when he saw a face he recognized. Lyle Sloan lay on a hospital bed with wraps around his torso and a bandage around his head. He was staring through the doorway at Slocum.

It was an opportunity Slocum couldn't resist.

He walked into the room and stood over the gunman's bed for a moment without saying a word. Sloan looked up at him with his lone good eye, but a change had come over his sinister countenance since they met in the room at Anna's. His face reflected the pain he suffered now.

"You picked the wrong man this time," Slocum said evenly, a bit of advice he enjoyed handing out after what Sloan did to the girl. "If you're ever able to walk again, I'd suggest you hang up your gun and look for another line of work. You ain't much at the gunfighter's trade."

"The hell with you, Slocum," Sloan croaked. "You got lucky this time."

"I've never counted on luck," he replied. "Being careful when it counts is better'n luck. You got careless at the wrong time."

Sloan looked away.

"Just one final warning," Slocum added, preparing to leave the room. "If anything ever happens to Miss Myra Reed, if she trips over a rock or even cuts her finger, I'll come looking for you and I'll finish it this time."

Sloan said nothing as he left the room.

He walked out as the sun climbed higher in the east, mounting his stud, reining northwest toward McLennan County. Just once, as he was riding away, he turned back for a look at the hospital, wondering if he might be leaving the best woman he'd met in quite a while.

Then he heeled the stallion to a trot and aimed for the edge of Austin, riding along the Colorado River before the road took him north.

Hell, he thought, he'd known plenty of good women over the years, a few that weren't so good. Leaving one behind was a part of his nature, something he doubted he could ever change.

22

He'd ridden by the Travis County Bank shortly after ten to pick up the money he'd had wired from his bank in Denver, more than enough to cover the bill he owed at the Driskell Hotel and for stabling his horse. But as he was riding his bay down Sixth Street, he saw Anna standing on the front porch of her establishment wearing a filmy night dress.

She waved him to a halt.

"Leaving town, John?"

He nodded. "Time I got back to Denver."

"Care for a cup of coffee before you go?"

He considered it. "I reckon I can spare the time. I've got an old friend in McLennan County I'd planned to visit on my way through."

"I put coffee on about half an hour ago. Climb down off that horse and I'll fix you a cup. Jory can see to your animal for a few minutes."

Slocum decided a short delay wouldn't make that much difference. He swung down and tied off his stallion at the picket fence around Anna's yard.

He walked inside, seeing the remnants of the handrail

on Anna's staircase where Younger's shotgun had blown it to pieces. Someone had mopped the bloodstains off her floor and cleaned her expensive rugs.

"You made a helluva mess of my place," she said, a tiny smile on her face. "Follow me to the kitchen."

"The mess couldn't be helped," he said. "I've never made a habit of lettin' another man shoot at me first."

"They were all bad men," she told him, directing to a table in a small kitchen at the rear of the place. "I shouldn't have allowed Lyle to bring that girl here . . . but Lyle was the kind who didn't like hearin' the word no."

Slocum took a chair. The big house was quiet, save for the soft bubbling of coffee on a cast iron woodstove. "I understand. Right now, he ain't hearing much of anything."

"Is he dead?"

"Doc Hardin told me he didn't expect him to live long. He said there was a lot of damage to his brain where I shot him in the head."

She poured Slocum's coffee into a china cup and set it before him. Then she stared at him a moment. "You're an amazing man, John Slocum, riding into town quiet as a church mouse, and then all of a sudden you start gunning down hired killers like you were on a duck hunt."

He shrugged. "They stuck their noses into my affairs an' I don't take that lightly."

Anna sat across from him, the front of her gown open just enough to give him a good view of the cleft between her breasts. "Tell me the truth, John. Somebody paid you to come to Austin to get rid of them. Am I right?"

"Nope. I was passing through, minding my own business. I'd never heard of Bob or Clay Younger or Lyle Sloan. I don't get down this way all that often."

"I don't believe you. It all happened too fast."

"It's the truth." He tasted his coffee and found it to his liking, almost as delicious as the time he spent in bed with Anna in order to find out where Myra was being kept.

It was as if she could read his mind. "You were only looking for the girl when you came upstairs with me."

"I did come here looking for Myra. A man told me this is where I'd find Sloan. But I'd be lyin' if I said you weren't a very pleasant distraction."

She smiled. "Would you like to be distracted again right now, before you left town?"

He didn't need long to consider it. Nothing pressing was pulling him toward McLennan County. A visit with an old friend could wait. "I'd find that downright delightful. You're quite a woman. A man would have to be a fool to turn down a chance like that."

"Drink your coffee. Then follow me upstairs. I promise you won't be disappointed."

He pushed the coffee cup aside. "I can get coffee most anywhere," he said. "Just lead the way."

She giggled girlishly. "You already know the way. Or have you forgotten so quickly?"

"I never forget a beautiful woman," he replied, pushing back his chair.

She escorted him out of the kitchen, her ample hips swaying.

As they neared the staircase, she spoke to him over her shoulder. "Watch out for this handrail, what's left of it. You might get a few splinters."

He rode up on a small ranch a few miles east of Bosqueville and recognized a lanky cowboy pushing a small herd of longhorn steers toward a set of pole corrals. The house wasn't much, a log affair, with a few cattle sheds behind it and a garden west of the cabin.

It'll be good to see Wayland again, he thought, counting the years, five or more.

Slocum heeled his bay to a short lope and rode toward the cowboy. He noticed right off that Wayland wasn't wearing a gun.

"Hey you!" Slocum bellowed, when he was in earshot. "I'm here to rustle this herd!"

Burke wheeled his buckskin gelding around, standing in his stirrups as he reached for a rifle booted to his saddle. "Like hell you are, stranger!" he cried.

Then Slocum threw back his head and started to laugh, and when he did, Burke booted his Winchester and smiled. "That just can't be you, John Slocum. I heard you was dead, or that you oughta be."

Both men were laughing hard as Slocum rode up to offer his handshake. "I thought I was dead myself a time or two, until I found out I'd just woke up next to a fat, ugly woman," Slocum replied.

"Damn you're a sight for sore eyes, John. How long has it been?"

"Five or six years, at least."

Burke let the steers wander while they talked. "What brings you this way?"

"Headed back to Denver. Bought some good horses an' now I need to sell 'em."

Burke grinned, reminding Slocum of the boyish grin he had during the war, even during the hard times those final months when they had no money or ammunition and precious little to eat, knowing they'd given four years to a losing cause.

"I've heard a few tales 'bout you from time to time," Burke said. "You earned yourself quite a name as a pistoleer, Johnny boy."

"You know how tales get blown up every time somebody else tells 'em."

"How come you didn't ride the train to Denver?"

"Just wanted to see some country, an' stop by so I could see if you're as ugly as you used to be."

Burke chuckled. "Just older, I reckon. I've got a missus now, an' two kids . . . a boy an' a girl. We'll pen the steers and then I want you to meet 'em. Beth will feed you good an' you'll bed down with us for the night. We've got a lot of catchin' up to do."

"Sounds mighty good to me. Can't wait to see a woman who's tough enough to have married you."

"She's real pretty, John, an' she don't know about all the women troubles we had back yonder. Better we talk about them some other time, when she ain't around."

"I understand," Slocum replied, moving his bay over behind a brindle steer to push it toward the corrals.

Burke grinned again. "I know damn well you ain't married. Did you find any pretty gals on the ride up?"

"I found two in Austin . . . a pretty young thing named Myra, and one of the prettiest women-for-hire I've seen in a helluva long time. Her name was Anna."

"Glad to hear you stayed out of trouble, Johnny boy. That ain't like you, not the way you used to be, anyhow."

"There was some trouble," Slocum recalled easily. "I had to kill three men down in Austin."

Burke jerked his gelding to a halt. "Then how come you ain't in jail?"

"They were gunslicks. The sheriff wouldn't face up to 'em, and the job sorta fell to me . . . on account of the girl. All of 'em drew on me first. The sheriff was relieved to be rid of 'em since he was scared to do it himself. One gent in particular had 'em all tucking their tails—a gunfighter named Lyle Sloan."

"You mean Red Sloan?" Burke asked, his face dark and serious now.

"Same one, I reckon."

"Damn, John," Burke said softly. "Red Sloan used to be the terror of north Fort Worth."

Slocum nudged his horse forward again. "He ain't any more. If he lives, he'll only see half his troubles. I put a bullet plumb through one of his eyes, then he fell out a two story window. Just before I left Austin, the doctor said he didn't think Sloan would live out the rest of the day."

Burke wagged his head as they neared the cattle pens with his steers. "Some feller's just don't change, John Slocum. I don't reckon you ever will."

J. R. ROBERTS
THE
GUNSMITH

__THE GUNSMITH #197:	APACHE RAID	0-515-12293-9/$4.99
__THE GUNSMITH #198:	THE LADY KILLERS	0-515-12303-X/$4.99
__THE GUNSMITH #199:	DENVER DESPERADOES	0-515-12341-2/$4.99
__THE GUNSMITH #200:	THE JAMES BOYS	0-515-12357-9/$4.99
__THE GUNSMITH #201:	THE GAMBLER	0-515-12373-0/$4.99
__THE GUNSMITH #202:	VIGILANTE JUSTICE	0-515-12393-5/$4.99
__THE GUNSMITH #203:	DEAD MAN'S BLUFF	0-515-12414-1/$4.99
__THE GUNSMITH #204:	WOMEN ON THE RUN	0-515-12438-9/$4.99
__THE GUNSMITH #205:	THE GAMBLER'S GIRL	0-515-12451-6/$4.99
__THE GUNSMITH #206:	LEGEND OF THE PIASA BIRD	
		0-515-12469-9/$4.99
__THE GUNSMITH #207:	KANSAS CITY KILLING	0-515-12486-9/$4.99
__THE GUNSMITH #208:	THE LAST BOUNTY	0-515-12512-1/$4.99
__THE GUNSMITH #209:	DEATH TIMES FIVE	0-515-12520-2/$4.99
__THE GUNSMITH #210:	MAXIMILIAN'S TREASURE	0-515-12534-2/$4.99
__THE GUNSMITH #211:	SON OF A GUNSMITH	0-515-12557-1/$4.99
__THE GUNSMITH #212:	FAMILY FEUD	0-515-12573-3/$4.99
__THE GUNSMITH #213:	STRANGLER'S VENDETTA	0-515-12615-2/$4.99
__THE GUNSMITH #214:	THE BORTON FAMILY GAME	
		0-515-12661-6/$4.99
__THE GUNSMITH #215:	SHOWDOWN AT DAYLIGHT	0-515-12688-8/$4.99
__THE GUNSMITH #216:	THE MAN FROM PECULIAR	0-515-12708-6/$4.99
__THE GUNSMITH #217:	AMBUSH AT BLACK ROCK	0-515-12735-3/$4.99
__THE GUNSMITH #218:	THE CLEVELAND CONNECTION	
		0-515-12756-6/$4.99
__THE GUNSMITH #219:	THE BROTHEL INSPECTOR	0-515-12771-X/$4.99
__THE GUNSMITH #220:	END OF THE TRAIL	0-515-12791-4/$4.99
__THE GUNSMITH #221:	DANGEROUS BREED	0-515-12809-0/$4.99

Prices slightly higher in Canada

Payable by Visa, MC or AMEX only ($10.00 min.), No cash, checks or COD. Shipping & handling: US/Can. $2.75 for one book, $1.00 for each add'l book; Int'l $5.00 for one book, $1.00 for each add'l. Call (800) 788-6262 or (201) 933-9292, fax (201) 896-8569 or mail your orders to:

Penguin Putnam Inc.
P.O. Box 12289, Dept. B
Newark, NJ 07101-5289
Please allow 4-6 weeks for delivery.
Foreign and Canadian delivery 6-8 weeks.

Bill my: ❑ Visa ❑ MasterCard ❑ Amex _____ (expires)

Card# _____

Signature _____

Bill to:

Name _____

Address _____ City _____

State/ZIP _____ Daytime Phone # _____

Ship to:

Name _____ Book Total $ _____

Address _____ Applicable Sales Tax $ _____

City _____ Postage & Handling $ _____

State/ZIP _____ Total Amount Due $ _____

This offer subject to change without notice.   Ad # 206 (8/00)